I0788182

BEAUTIFUL BLADE

A BEAUTY AND THE BEAST ROMANTASY NOVELLA

THE LUNATERRA CHRONICLES
BOOK EIGHT

INES JOHNSON

THOSE JOHNSON GIRLS

CHAPTER ONE

JORGE

Nine years old

The scent of damp hay and something fouler —rot or mildew, perhaps—burned my nostrils as I clung on to the back of the rickety wooden carriage. The uneven wheels jostled by every uneven groove of the cobbled road as the gredane picked its way down the path.

"Move, you lazy beast," Uncle Maris snapped.

I jolted, assuming he was talking to me. But there

was nothing for me to do in the wagon but hold on. It was the gredane that had caught his ire.

Gredanes were relics on the planet of Lunaterra. Much like pure-blooded humans. The animal's sheer size was a reminder of the majestic beasts humans had brought to Lunaterra when they'd arrived thousands of years ago. Its coat was a checkered pattern of black and white blocks splashed across its massive body. The pattern was beautiful, even in the animal's patchy and worn state. A large black spot encircled one of its droopy eyes, giving it a look of perpetual sadness. Its joints clicked, and a tremble ran through its legs as it pulled the rickety cart forward.

Uncle Maris yanked the reins. The gredane stumbled. It howled miserably at the jerk of its master.

I hated that sound. It always made my stomach twist. My fingers curled into the edge of the splintered cart as we came to a stop.

The strap at Uncle's waist came loose, dangling like a coiled snake as he climbed down from the driver's seat. He stomped toward the gredane, muttering curses under his breath.

Uncle Maris raised the whip high. The gredane's ears flattened as its large, watery eyes squeezed shut, bracing for the strike. It wasn't the blow itself that broke the beast. It was the waiting that did it. The strike was always quick. The waiting stretched the attack out.

The whip rose in the air like a bowstring being pulled taut. My eyes darted to the worn and cracked metal shoe encasing the gredane's left paw.

"Wait." The word tumbled out before I could stop it.

Uncle froze, the whip hanging in the air like a dark omen. He turned slowly, his sharp, beady eyes fixing on me with a look that made my blood run cold. "What did you just say, boy?"

"Something's wrong—down there. The shoe. It's loose. I—I can fix it. If it's loose, I can fix it."

There was silence except for the faint rustle of wind through the trees. The anticipation grew thick as I waited for the verdict. The bow stretched tauter and tauter. The string would snap once the blow fell across my cheek. Or the gredane's. Right now, the animal and I were both experiencing the pain of the wait, and I just wanted it to end.

Uncle Maris dropped the whip to his side, but the relief I felt was short-lived. He yanked the reins with one hand, jerking the gredane's head violently to the side. The beast stumbled, letting out a miserable howl.

"Fix it quick. We can't be late for their royal flowernesses."

Uncle ambled to a watering hole off the main road. He unlaced his britches and relieved himself on the bark of a tree, not in the stream. This was fairy land, a place where flowers and trees were sentient. The blades of grass bristled at the disrespect.

I scooted to the edge of the cart, trying to drop myself slowly to the ground. The moment I touched the earth, my feet were kicked out from beneath me. With my legs already weak, I couldn't mount a quick defense. Not that my gangly arms and legs were any defense to begin with.

Olric had his father's whip in his hand. He lashed out before I could scramble back. I had no time to anticipate the strike. The sting made me gasp from the pain. It was sharp and hot, a burning coal against my skin.

"Think you're smarter than my Da, you crackling?"

He struck again. This time, the whip caught my arm. The brittle bones inside gave a cracking protest, like dry twigs snapping underfoot.

"You don't tell my Da how to handle his own beast, you little twiglet."

Tears sprang to my eyes. I didn't dare let any fall. I bit down hard on my lip, trying to keep from crying out. It was like a game. If I didn't cry, maybe he'd stop sooner.

It worked. Olric dropped the strap. It fell into Dain's hand.

Dain was the taller of the two. Uncle Maris had married an orc. His spawn had gotten her strength and nothing else. Dain understood the suffering of anticipation, having met his father's blows on a regular basis. He made me wait, feinting a few times before delivering a series of blows.

Olric sneered, his boot slamming into my ribs. I curled up on the ground, clutching my stomach as Dain laughed.

"Look at him squirm. He's like a bug, he is." Dain aimed another kick at my gut.

I was sure I'd pass out. But then, just as suddenly as it started, it stopped. The two wandered off, laughing as they headed over to the water's edge with their father. Uncle Maris unwrapped a lunch of stale bread and bruised fruit. I didn't bother to join them. I knew I'd get nothing but scraps. And that's if I was lucky.

Something warm and wet brushed my face. I flinched, expecting more pain. When I opened my eyes, the gredane stood over me. Its huge, droopy ears twitched. Its tongue darted out to lick the side of my face.

Wincing, I tried to sit up. My ribs screamed in protest, but I managed to pat the beast's nose. "You're welcome. But you have to pick up the pace now."

The gredane huffed softly, a sound almost like a sigh, as it licked at my wounds. I let it offer me comfort, since nothing could heal my weak human frame. Where the gredane had lost its strength due to its age, I was a young creature born fragile, my bones as brittle as dry twigs. They broke easily with even the smallest strain, and though they healed quickly thanks to the magic that was in the very atmosphere of the planet, they always grew back weaker, thinner, more breakable than before.

I walked with a limp from an injury that had never properly mended when I was five solars old. My thin arms struggled to carry even a sack of grain. No amount of rest or care could make me strong. Not as if Uncle Maris or his sons, whose blows always felt like thunder striking stone, ever gave me space to rest.

By the time the mother sun had set and the daughter sun had led the thirteen moons on their nightly chase across the skies, we arrived at our destination. The fairy manor rose like a dream from the heart of the lush garden. No metal marred its beauty— only wood, glass, and vines woven into intricate patterns blending seamlessly with the surrounding flora.

Pale blue luminara blossoms unfurled their petals in the cool night air, each one glowing faintly like tiny stars scattered across the ground. Climbing vines of moonsilk wove themselves along the wooden beams of the manor, their silvery blooms spilling down like waterfalls of light. Nearby, beds of whispering lilies swayed gently, as if moved by an unseen breeze, their petals tinged with iridescent hues that shifted whenever they caught the light.

The air was heavy with the intoxicating perfume of etherrose, a flower with deep violet petals and faintly glowing veins of gold running through them. Beneath the canopy of flowering trees, clusters of dewshade orchids nestled in the shadows, their pale green blossoms dripping with nectar that glittered like tiny jewels.

Tree branches arched protectively over the manor, the rustle of their leaves a melodic whispering of secrets to the wind. Moonweaver oaks stood sentinel around the grounds, their bark smooth and white as marble. Lantern-like fruits hung from their branches, their soft golden glow casting dappled patterns on the pathways below.

The village as well as the manor were all long asleep. My uncle and cousins headed inside to the servants' quarters and were greeted by a haggard-looking fae who looked down his long nose at them. Many faekind considered themselves the most evolved lifeforms on a planet with two suns made for beings who took sustenance from light and thrived in fertile grounds. They tolerated shifters, looked down their noses at orcs, and gave no attention whatsoever to humans.

Without being told to, I took the gredane to the stables. She moved slowly, her massive frame trembling with each step, her hooves clanging hollowly against the cobbled path. The shoes she wore were old and heavy, their crude edges biting into the soft flesh just above her hoofed paw despite the work I'd just done to them to get us here.

My fingers brushed the rough metal. An idea sparked in my mind—a better shoe, one that could take the burden off her legs. Something lighter, curved to fit perfectly, and lined with a soft material that wouldn't leave bruises. The thought stayed with me as I found a second blanket, one not too marred by dirt and feces. Dragging it into the stall beside hers, I bedded down for the night, my head full of designs and possibilities.

I had to admit the stable was nicer than the last place I'd slept in. There was hay beneath my back instead of stone. My ribs still ached from the beating, and every movement sent a sharp reminder of my cousins' attentions. The hay scratched against my back as I tried to get comfortable, the earthy smell of it mingling with the sharp tang of manure and the faint sweetness of the flowers outside. The night was calm now, the kind of calm that made the world seem like it had forgotten you entirely.

I don't know how long I lay there, staring at the wooden beams above me, before I heard it—the faint creak of the stable door opening again.

I bolted upright, ignoring the way my ribs screamed

at the movement. I expected Olric or Dain. They some-times liked a late night kick to my shins before they could settle down and go to sleep. But it was neither of my cousins.

A figure slipped inside, cloaked in shadow except for the faint glow of a lantern held high in one hand. The light threw her face into soft relief—a small, heart-shaped face, partially hidden by the hood of a dark cloak.

I froze, unsure whether to speak or stay silent. Her movements were light and deliberate, like she didn't want to wake the sleeping world. At first, I thought she might be a servant from the manor. Maybe she'd come to check on the other animals. Maybe Uncle had sent her to make sure I hadn't run off.

As she moved closer, the lantern light revealed something that made my breath catch. Her skin—it wasn't pale or sun-bronzed like mine and the other human farmers or workers I'd seen on our journey into the kingdom of Evergrove. It wasn't the fertile brown of my father's people, either. No, her skin shimmered faintly in the light, soft and smooth as polished stone but unmistakably lavender. A pale, delicate purple like the petals of the whispering lilies in the manor gardens.

She set the lantern down on a barrel near the door and reached up to undo the clasp of her cloak. The fabric fell away, and I saw them—her wings.

They unfurled, shimmering with an iridescent glow that caught every sliver of moonlight sneaking through the wooden slats of the stable. They looked delicate, like spun glass. The way they moved—strong and purposeful—made me think they were anything but fragile.

She pulled a crystal tablet from her satchel, its glassy surface smooth and faintly glowing with inner light. With a flick of her fingers, the glow intensified, and images sprang to life, casting the stable in flickering shades of gold and blue. The sights and sounds of the Convergence Games filled the air—roaring crowds, clashing weapons, and the rhythmic pounding of drums that set the pace for the combatants.

Her eyes lit up as the fighters appeared on the crystal's surface. It was the Sun and Moon Gauntlet, where competitors faced a series of elemental and magical barriers before facing each other in hand-to-hand combat. The fairy stepped back, holding a—was that a steak knife?—in one hand, and began mimicking the movements of the fighters. She swung an imaginary sword, ducked low, and lunged forward with a sharp thrust.

I couldn't stop the gasp that escaped me.

She froze, her head snapping toward me. Her wide eyes found mine. Neither of us moved.

The crystal flickered while the announcer's voice

continued narrating the battle happening live in the capital of Solmane. The fairy girl aimed her dull blade at my gut.

In this anticipation, I felt no fear. For the first time in my short life, I felt excitement.

"Who are you?" she demanded.

CHAPTER TWO

CHARLOTTE

"Who are you?" I asked the man of my dreams.

"I'm yours," he told me with a cheeky smile before he disappeared under my skirts.

I squirmed in my seat, letting my thighs fall open wide, wider for him to fit his whole face in between—

"Charlotte, sit up straight. We are not wilting vines on the side of a butchery."

I blinked out of my daydream and sat up straight. Not because my mother told me to. Because my brain strained to work out what she meant. Queen Indira had never once been to a butchery in her life. She wouldn't know if it had vines on the outside walls or not.

The carriage jostled again. I felt the familiar prickle of discomfort between my shoulder blades. My wings were folded tightly beneath the fabric of my dress, pressed so firmly that I could barely draw a full breath. The binding wasn't meant to keep me in line. It was meant to protect others from the sight of me.

A fairy's wings were a weakness for most males. The sight of them bared was apparently too much for their fragile wills. A man might drop his trousers and commit fornication at the sight of them. All of which would be the fairy's fault, of course. Not the male's. It was always the damsel's fault that she stepped into danger by moving through her ordinary world.

I hated my ordinary world. But I knew better than to fall back into my daydream under my mother's watchful eyes. So instead, I pressed my forehead against the cool glass of the window and watched the landscape blur past.

Fields of wildflowers stretched out to the horizon, golden under the light of the mother-daughter suns. Solara bathed the earth in her steady, maternal warmth, while her daughter Lyra cast her fiery red glow over the edges of the sky. I envied Lyra's freedom. When her mother's back was turned, she could burn as brightly as she wanted.

"Charlotte, fix your posture. You're slouching like a common kitchen maid."

Another reference my mother had no clue about. But that was my mother. The Fairy Queen of Evermore often spoke of things she had no direct knowledge of.

Charlotte, you are the luckiest girl in the world to be marrying the prince of Solmane. But did she know all the girls in the world? Had she or anyone from the land asked any of the other girls if they wanted to marry a prince?

Charlotte, why are you wearing blue when you know that Prince Adom's favorite color is red? Was it red? Not that I actually cared what my betrothed's favorites were.

The point was my mother had never actually asked the prince. She'd never met him. Neither had I. That would all change tonight. Not that I had a say in it.

"When we get there, you will not say anything unless asked by the prince. You will sit straight. You will smile. You will charm your betrothed."

How was I supposed to charm someone without saying anything to them? Oh right, my mistake. Once again, I thought someone might want to know my opinion. Only one person in this world had ever asked my opinion.

"What do you think of this thread, your highness?"

Okay, two people. Belle, the seamstress, had asked about my likes for each stitch of the wedding dress she was making for me. The problem there was that I didn't care about the dress. I didn't want to get married. Not to the Beast Prince, anyway.

Not because he was rumored to look like a monster. I wasn't one to judge. I just wanted to be asked. Had I been asked, I would've told everyone with ears to hear that my heart had been stolen when I was just nine years old.

"I defer to your opinion, Belle. You know more about such things than I do."

Belle offered a smile. It was a smile that said she wasn't buying it. But she didn't voice her concerns. There were times I wished I could count her as a friend, that I could tell her my opinions. That I could tell another soul that I'd lost my heart, but I had a plan to get it back. Just a few more hours, and I'd enact my plan to find my lost heart and make all right in my world again.

"We could let the pegasuses fly instead of walking on land like common steeds," I suggested. Anything to get us to Pridehaven, the capitol of Solmane quicker.

"If we flew, then we would not be seen."

"That makes no sense, Mother. We don't want to appear like peasants, but we want the peasants to see us?"

"Exactly. We are to be seen and heard, like any good little princess."

Both Belle and I bit our lips. We didn't get many visitors in Evergrove. This would be both mine and Belle's first adventure out of our small municipality. Like me, Belle had big plans. When I wore the wedding gown in front of all of Solmane, she would become a fashion icon. It was too bad I was going to ruin those plans for her.

"Relax, Belle. The Beast Prince won't care if there's a wrinkle in the gown. He'll be too busy ripping it off me on our wedding night."

"Enough, Charlotte." Mother snapped her lily-white fingers in a controlled gesture of disapproval. "You have been training for this since the day you were born."

"You know who else trains since the day they're born? Warriors in the Convergence Games. Except if they don't pass muster, they die."

"You won't die. Not if you behave yourself."

I had been behaving myself for the last three years. I'd had no choice in that matter, either. There had been a contingent of Sky Keeper guards living at Evergrove manor to ensure my safety. The truth was, they were ensuring I didn't make a run for it. Had their eyes not been on my every move, I would've made my escape far sooner than my latest plan.

"Charlotte, fix your dress. Your wings are showing. Do you want Her Lioness to think you're some flaming Ember Fae?"

"Yes, Mother," I replied, my voice flat. I did want the Lioness to think I was some Ember Fae. Then maybe she would think I wasn't good enough for her son.

The carriage jerked to a halt, throwing me forward. My hands flew to the window, bracing myself as I muttered a curse under my breath.

"What now?" I hissed, craning my neck to see outside.

The golden fields that had blurred into oblivion moments ago were now still, stretching endlessly beneath the two suns. The faint sound of voices reached my ears. The carriage door opened. Sunlight spilled inside, momentarily blinding me.

A man stood there, tall and poised, the very embodiment of servitude carved into flesh. His face was all sharp angles and precise lines, as if sculpted by someone who valued utility over beauty. High cheekbones gave him an almost regal air, but the severity of his expression undercut any warmth. Pale blond hair was pulled back with meticulous care, each strand so perfectly in place that it seemed almost unnatural, as though his appearance itself was a performance.

But it was his eyes that held my attention—gray as storm clouds, cool and unreadable. He was a man who understood his place and played his role with precision, never saying too much, never doing too little. The kind of person who could anticipate needs before they were spoken and quietly act on them without drawing attention to himself.

"Greetings, your royal highnesses. I am Colson, Chamberlain of Pridehaven Palace. Prince Adom has charged me with escorting you to the summer castle."

"The summer castle?" said my mother. "We were told to arrive at the palace."

"Yes, Highness. However, the prince is waiting inside the summer castle, which is just down this road. He wishes to greet his bride in private before entering the palace grounds."

A private meeting with the Beast Prince. The words churned in my stomach like spoiled nectar. That was not how I'd planned for this to go. I had planned never to set eyes on the Beast Prince.

"Princess Charlotte would be delighted to have a rendezvous with her betrothed," my mother was saying.

Chamberlain Colson gave a polite bow. The door to the carriage shut, and we were moving again. The moment we were out of hearing distance from the Chamberlain, the queen's calm façade dropped.

"Fix her. Now."

I ignored my mother as she hurled commands at Belle. I ignored Belle as she got to work on me. The seamstress was handy with more than clothes. Her magic could also trim nails and remove dirt from the body or clothes.

Belle and my mother could remove all the dirt they wanted. I was busy working on another plan.

I had known this day was coming all my life. My twenty-first birthday was in just two days on the Hunter's Eclipse. That was the day the death blow would strike and my life would be over.

I had been waiting for this day. The anticipation of it had been the worst thing. Now that it was happening, I was pure reaction.

My initial plan had changed, but not my goal. I was closer to the city. I was closer to him. I just had to get free of my mother and this carriage, not go into the summer castle where my betrothed was waiting for me, get to the Convergence Games, and find him.

I'm yours, I heard him say in my ears, in my head, in my heart. It was the only truth I knew. He was mine, and I was going to get him back.

CHAPTER THREE

JORGE

Twelve years old

The stables smelled of clean hay, leather, and the musk of pegasus. It was a good smell, familiar and grounding in a way few things were. I crouched by Silverfoot, the oldest of the herd, and lifted his hoof, resting the weight of his leg against my knee. His silver coat shimmered in the filtered light that trickled through the gaps in the stable walls.

"Easy, boy. I'll fix it. Just hold still."

I ran my thumb along the edge of the lightweight metal shoe fixed to his hoof. The design was something I'd first created for the gredane, a way to ease their burden and give them more traction during long journeys. It curved to fit perfectly against the hoof and lined with a soft material that absorbed the impact. The pegasuses had taken to it just as naturally as the gredane, their wings catching less strain because of the even weight distribution.

For some reason, metal yielded to me. It listened to me. Sometimes I thought the material might even like me.

"There. All better."

I patted Silverfoot's flank, and the animal flinched. Bruises, dark and angry, mottled the delicate membrane of his wings. Farther up, small rashes fanned out where the harness rubbed too tightly against his skin.

I moved down the row of stalls, inspecting the others. They weren't much better off. I found more bruising, chafing, even small cuts where the straps had dug too deeply into flesh that was never meant to bear the strain of cargo.

Leaning against the stall door, I stared at the pile of discarded harnesses in the corner. Most were made of heavy leather. They dug into the wings, forcing the weight onto one part of the body. That was the problem. The weight wasn't balanced. It was all concentrated in one place.

What if I made the harness of lighter material? Metal—no, not just any metal. A lighter alloy, one that wouldn't cut into their wings or strain their muscles. I pictured it in my mind, a frame that curved around the body, distributing the weight more evenly. Something sleek, something that could let the air flow over their wings without resistance.

The idea took root, growing with each second. It would need padding, something soft to protect their skin. Straps that didn't bind, that could flex and move with the rhythm of their flight. I'd seen the way they moved, how their wings beat in harmony with their bodies. The design would have to honor that—work with them, not against them.

"Poor Princess Charlotte. Betrothed to the Beast Prince."

"Better a beast than some human. Did you know that, in the south, Revenants are just as likely to sacrifice human brides as they are to marry them?"

"They marry humans? The cold of being in the south pole of the planet must addle their brains."

"Come on, we're done with this birthday party. If we're quick, we'll catch Drakos' bout in the Convergence Games. I heard he's fighting with a mech fist this year."

"He'll lay Rip Vander flat with it."

I remained in the shadows of the stables, out of sight. Fairy boys were worse than my cousins. The maids would halfheartedly reprimand Olric and Dain when they got their hands on me. They would turn a blind eye to any fairy who did.

Outside, the faint red hue of the Hunter's Moon bled across the sky, the eclipse casting Avarix into a bloody darkness as Lunaterra moved between Lyra and the first moon. The eerie light bathed everything in crimson, making the shadows deeper and the air heavier.

The fae boys darted across the darkening fields and into the woods. Once they were out of sight, I ducked into the forge. Inside, the air was thick and hot, alive with the scent of soot, iron, and oil. I stoked the embers until the flames roared to life, golden and hungry.

My uncle wasn't present. He'd likely be flat on his back in the cottage shared with his sons, an empty bottle on his bedside table. Goddess knew where his sons were. They could slack off because they knew I'd get all of their work done without complaint.

I wouldn't complain. Not when their absence granted me the space and time for my task. I'd been waiting all day for this moment—this chance to work on my project.

The dagger lay waiting for me on the workbench. The blade was simple, but the design was elegant. Vines coiled sinuously up the hilt, their etched lines winding like living tendrils. Tiny blooms erupted along their length, each petal painstakingly detailed to resemble the soft, layered folds of lavender flowers.

At the base of the hilt, I was planning to add a cluster of blossoms before wrapping the handle in a purple leather to echo her lavender skin. I ran my fingers along the spine, the metal humming softly in response to my touch. It wanted to be finished. It wanted to be presented to her.

I turned back to the flames with the dagger in hand. The heat kissed my skin as I worked. The clang of my hammer rang against the blade like a song. My arms ached, my bad shoulder burning with each strike, but I didn't stop.

"What is that?"

Her voice startled me like a bolt of lightning through the dark. I jerked, the hammer slipping from my grip. The dagger dropped from my hand. In my clumsy attempt to catch it, the blade skimmed across my palm. Pain flared sharp and bright as I hissed, stumbling back and clutching my hand.

Charlotte grabbed my hand. And just like that, I

forgot the sting. Just looking at her made any ache, any weakness in my bones melt away.

To me, she was pure magic.

The gash on my palm was red and angry-looking. A bead of blood dripped onto the floor. I winced as she turned it over, inspecting it. Her fingers brushed my skin. The pain dulled. The cut closed. The warmth of her touch chased away the worst of the sting.

"You're hopeless, Jorge." She tugged a strip of cloth from her cloak and wiped away any evidence that I'd been hurt. "How do you survive on your own?"

"I don't. You're the one always saving me."

Her touch was careful as she tied off the bandage. I swallowed hard, watching the way her fingers moved. For someone who claimed she had no skill for practical things, Charlotte was always gentle with me. Always careful.

"You shouldn't be here. It's your birthday. You should be... celebrating."

"You know I hate this day. If I'd only held on inside my mother's womb for a few more hours, I would have a different life. I swear I think she pushed me out on this cursed eclipse on purpose."

The bandage was tied, but she didn't release my hand. Her fingers idly twined with mine. Her numbing magic seeped into my knuckles, into my fingertips, into every crevice of my being that was lonely.

"You didn't answer my question. What is that?"

I bent to pick up the blade up, wincing as the movement tugged at my shoulder. "It's for you. It's your birthday present."

"For me?" Her eyes lit up as she leaned closer, the light catching on the silver sheen of the blade. "It's beautiful." Then, as if realizing herself, she reached out to touch it—only to snatch her hand back at the last moment.

"It's not iron. It's something I've been experimenting with. A synthetic. It'll be as tough as steel. You'll be able to wield it."

Charlotte gave me that smile, the one that had made my heart come to a full stop three years ago when we first met. The one that had given notice that I was no longer the owner of the organ inside my chest.

"Do you know what everyone else gave me today? Things befitting a future queen. Things they think the Beast Prince would like. None of those gifts were for me. They were for the princess they think I'm supposed to be. But you… you gave me something I wanted. Something my heart desired."

My throat felt tight, and I looked away, focusing on the dagger. "It's just a blade."

"It's from you. You always think about me."

She had no idea how right she was about that. I

thought about Charlotte every waking moment. She was in my dreams, too.

"You're my best friend, Jorge."

"You're my only friend, Charlotte."

"I don't have any real friends either. Everyone wants something from me. My favor. My power—not that I have any. They all want me to pretend to be someone I'm not."

"You don't have to pretend with me."

She looked at me for a long moment, her blue eyes searching mine as though trying to find something. Then she smiled again—smaller this time, but no less genuine. "I know. That's why you're my favorite person in the entire world."

The forge glowed faintly, the last of the fire crackling low in its stone belly, like an animal reluctant to sleep. I wiped the sweat from my brow with the back of my sleeve. I needed a moment without the full force of her. The fire in her would eat me alive, and I would happily add more kindling to my funeral pyre.

"I managed to get away just in time for Drakos and Rip Vander's match." Charlotte clutched a crystal viewer in her hands. Its glowing surface pulsed with the promise of the Games. "I can't believe he succumbed and got a mech hand."

"You don't approve of mechanical enhancements?"

"I'm a fairy. Metal isn't my thing."

"It could make him stronger."

"I like my fighters natural." She grinned. "Let's head to the stables to watch."

"I'll be right there," I said, gesturing toward the fire. "Just let me put this out."

Her hand moved toward the dagger. Her fingers brushed the hilt. The metal hummed beneath her touch, as though it recognized her, as though it knew it had always belonged to her. She ran her thumb over the flowery engravings, a small, private smile pulling at her lips.

Then, without warning, she turned and leaned in, pressing a chaste kiss to my cheek. Her lips were warm, just the barest brush of skin against mine. It sent a jolt straight to my chest like I'd touched pure starlight.

She pulled back, and her blue eyes met mine—wide and startled, as though she hadn't quite thought it through. The space between us felt different now, tighter, charged. Neither of us moved.

Charlotte blinked, her face blanking into a serene mask, as though the moment hadn't happened at all. "Hurry up, or you're going to miss it," she said, backing toward the door. "I want to see who makes it to the next round, and I'm not recapping anything you miss."

Then she was gone, her laughter floating back toward me as she sprinted for the stables. I stood there, staring at the empty doorway, the echo of her kiss still burning on my cheek.

My heart beat hard and uneven. I pressed my palm to my chest to steady it. It was hopeless. The word rolled through my head like a stone.

It was hopeless to dream. I was human—weak, breakable, and unremarkable in the eyes of a world where fairies lived like royalty and I belonged in the dirt. Charlotte would marry the Beast Prince. She would become the queen of Solmane.

That didn't change what I felt.

My heart had belonged to her since the first day I saw her, wild and defiant, standing in the shadow of the stables, practicing a kick like her favorite warrior, Kael Drakos. I'd spent the last three years learning how to be of use to her—how to make her smile when no one else could, how to fix the little things no one else noticed.

I'd go with her when she left for the palace, some-how. I'd find a way to stay at her side, to be the one who asked what she wanted, what she needed. I'd make sure someone saw her—not the princess, but Charlotte.

I turned back to the forge, my hands moving auto-matically as I doused the flames. The recognition of the sound of boots behind me came too late. A rough hand shoved me forward, slamming me into the workbench. My ribs hit the edge of the table. Pain bloomed through my side.

"Playing with fire again, little crackling?"

"Is that a weapon? What's a twiglet like you doing with something like that?"

I wanted to reach for the dagger but knew that if I showed how precious it was that it would then be lost to me. But I wasn't in my right mind today, not after Charlotte's kiss. I was also feeling stronger with her healing magic in the palm of my hand. So I reached for the dagger.

"Careful, Olric. He might poke you with it."

The laughter that followed made my fists clench. Olric took a step forward. His large shadow swallowed the faint light of the forge.

I didn't think. I just moved. The hilt of the dagger was solid in my palm, the blade an extension of me. I swung it upward, and the edge caught Olric's forearm. He yelped, stumbling back as the blade left a thin, red line across his skin.

"You little—" Olric roared.

I didn't hear any more. Both of them were on me. I hit the floor hard, the dagger knocked from my grip as fists pummeled my ribs, my arms, my face. My body screamed in protest, my bones aching under the assault.

"Stop!"

In all my years with my uncle and his demon spawn, I'd never dared utter that word. No one had: not my uncle, not the other workers standing around or turning a blind eye. So when that word sounded in the middle of the whacks and thumps, it rang through the forge like a thunderclap. The beating stopped abruptly.

I cracked one swollen eye open just in time to see Charlotte standing in the doorway. Her blue eyes blazed with fury, her shoulders squared like a warrior's. Her unfinished birthday blade gleamed dangerously in her hand.

"Get off him." Charlotte's voice was low and deadly.

Olric's face paled. "We weren't—we didn't—"

"Now." The tip of the dagger gleamed as she held it out.

Dain and Olric scrambled back, stumbling over themselves in their haste. Olric glared at her, but he didn't dare say anything. Not to a fairy princess.

"Run to your father," Charlotte said coldly. "Tell him you're all dismissed."

The threat landed, and they slunk out of the forge, casting one last venomous glare my way before disappearing out the door.

Charlotte knelt beside me, her face softening as she looked me over. "Jorge? Are you all right?"

I tried to sit up. Pain flared through my ribs. "You can't do that. You can't dismiss my uncle. He'll take me away from you."

"No one will take you away from me. You are mine." The dagger lay beside her. The firelight caught the sharp edge as though it backed up her words. "I mean, you belong to the manor. I'll tell my mother. It will all be fine."

Her hands were gentle as she helped me sit up. Her fingers brushed against my bruised skin. At her touch, the bruising went quiet, the pain silent. As if the agony didn't dare linger in the wake of her touch, as if her presence alone demanded my body to stop its protest and simply feel… good.

"Don't waste your power on me."

"I won't leave you in pain."

The ache that had lodged itself deep inside me began to dissolve, replaced by a warmth that spread outward like sunlight on dissolving morning dew. Charlotte's wasn't the kind of healing that mended torn flesh or stitched gaping wounds. The pain didn't fade because I was healed; it faded because she willed it to. She was a drug, and I had to remember that my body was still injured despite feeling numb. Every part of me felt alive, hyper-aware of her proximity, of her hands, her scent, her voice.

And that was the danger, wasn't it? Pain was the body's way of announcing that something was wrong. Charlotte was a descendant of poppies, flowers renowned for their soothing properties, able to lull even the sharpest pain into a gentle stupor. My injuries weren't life-threatening, just a nuisance. A nuisance she'd ensured wouldn't bother me while they healed.

"Now are you coming or not? We've already missed the opening ceremony."

I took her hand. The bandage had come away, leaving the wound exposed. Charlotte pressed her palm to mine. The jagged scar protested. I ignored it. The moment her flesh met mine, all the hurt went happily silent. Our fingers remained linked all the way to the stables.

CHAPTER FOUR

CHARLOTTE

"*D*o something with the nails and makeup. The prince likes red." With that, my mother descended from the carriage in a flurry of silk and lilies. Her floral scent lingered in the air, her anthers seeming to pollinate the space with a silent reprimand.

Belle turned to me. Her green eyes were apologetic as she reached for my hands.

I pulled them away. "I can't do this."

"I can give you a quick manicure. It will all be fine."

I reached for the door on the other side of the carriage. My mother was already disappearing into the castle's darkened doors. I got out and began walking toward the stone walls that surrounded the castle. The doors to the outside world were closed. No one manned the massive battlements to reopen it.

"I can't do it, Belle. I won't."

I was starting to crack. I'd known this day was coming. It was one of my first memories, because it had been told to me over and over again every day of my life. *I was going to marry the Beast Prince on my twenty-first birthday.* That was in just two days.

"I can't marry that beast."

"I'm sure the rumors are an exaggeration. He's the son of a lioness. So he might have a big nose and sharp teeth. It's not like he's a troll."

Belle wasn't listening to me. I didn't expect her to. No one ever listened to me. No one except him.

There was a chance he was here. If he was, I would find him. I didn't know that he would still have me. He'd promised. But I'd promised, too, and I'd broken my end of the bargain on the day that he was taken from me. I would not fail him again.

I looked around, this time realizing that I was practically alone. The Sky Keeper Mage guards who had been dogging my steps since I was eighteen were all gone. The moment they'd stepped onto the beast's grounds, they'd finally laid down their arms and took their gazes from me. There was no one stopping me from running this time.

I gathered the edges of my skirt and bolted for the wall. My boots struck the ground with sharp, frantic sounds. My hands reached for the lattice as though it were salvation.

"Your Highness," Belle called, the panic rising in her throat. "Stop!"

I didn't stop. I climbed. I hefted my leg up and over the wall. There was a scrape of metal against stone. It was the blade he'd made me all those years ago. The intricate designs on the metal were a series of inter-twining flowers he'd finished at the same time as we watched the closing ceremonies of that year's Conver-gence Games.

Everyone thought I was dainty, fragile—delicate was the word the fairy court liked to use, as though my lavender skin and princess-cut gowns defined me. They had no idea. Those gowns didn't define me, they hid the truth.

I'd been training for this moment since I was nine years old, when I first realized no one was coming to save me. I didn't have a delicate bone in my body. The muscles on my arms and legs had been forged by that fire as Jorge had worked. I had been getting stronger as he'd made me weapons to train with. By the time I was eighteen, I'd mapped our escape, every last detail, down to the weight of my boots and the blade I'd strapped to my thigh.

My nails bit into the cracks of the stone wall as I hauled myself up. I wouldn't say it was easy, not with my arms burning with the strain. The wind tugged at the edges of my dress, trying to pull me back. I set my jaw and kept going.

The stones were cold beneath my hands, slick in places. Twice my foot slipped. The second time, I scrapped my knee but caught myself. A delicate princess would have cried out. I gritted my teeth through the sting and pressed on like the warrior I was.

The only reason I'd been obedient these past few years—the perfect little princess, docile and well-dressed—was because they'd sent him to the capital. He'd looked me in the eye the day they dragged him away and promised to survive. I trusted that he'd kept that promise. Now, I was going to find him.

"Charlotte, please."

I looked down at Belle. It struck me then how much we favored each other. Same pale lavender skin, same dark indigo hair. She looked regal holding my wedding gown in her arms. I'm sure I looked like something off the street with my legs thrown over a wall.

I'd only had one friend all my life. One person who

had looked out for me. The dressmaker had tried in her way. I wish we could've had more time.

Maybe we could've been friends. But she was not my destiny. Neither was the Beast Prince. Today, I was going to take my life in the direction I chose.

"I don't want this life, Belle." And with that, I jumped.

The wind rushed past my ears, a sharp, whistling cry that ended with a thud as I landed. I rolled onto the grass to absorb the fall. The impact jolted through my bones, leaving me breathless. I pushed up onto my knees, my hands digging into the dirt. For the first time all day, I smiled in earnest.

Freedom.

I rose to my feet, brushing dirt off my skirt as I glanced around. The forest stretched out endlessly—fields of tall grass and opposing treetops rippling in the wind like waves on the sea. A faint path wound toward the main road. I turned away from it immediately. If I took that route, they'd catch me before midnight.

No, I'd have to go through the forest.

I broke into a run. Each step sent a small thrill through me, a defiant surge that drowned out the voice in my head whispering I'd never make it. My breath came hard and fast. The wind snatched at my cloak, but I pressed on, racing against the dying light of the day.

I paused just inside the tree line, my hands braced

on my knees as I sucked in lungfuls of air. The first stars blinked to life above me. Slowly, the first moon began to rise.

Avarix's pale light spilled across the treetops, cold and judgmental. He had always been the watcher, the oldest of the moons. When the people of Lunaterra bent their heads to him, it was in obedience to the will of fate.

But I wasn't going to obey. Not this time.

I glared up at the moon, its silver face half-shrouded in shadow, and felt a chill seep into my bones. I would defy him. I would find my own way.

The moon glared back at me, as if he disapproved of my rebellion. His light dimmed as I moved deeper into the forest. The shadows grew thicker, swallowing the faint path ahead.

The deeper I went, the darker it became. Avarix's light didn't follow me. It stayed behind, as though turning its back. I strained my eyes to see. The shadows were pitch black, pressing in on all sides.

I heard the creak of branches above me, the soft rustle of unseen creatures moving through the under-brush. A branch snapped, close enough to send ice straight through my veins. I froze, my heart lurching painfully against my ribs.

I was not alone.

The silence that followed was deafening. I couldn't

see anything, couldn't hear anything beyond my own ragged breath. But I felt it—something watching me.

My hand moved instinctively to my thigh, where the dagger Jorge had made me was strapped. My fingers curled around the hilt, comforted by its cool weight as I waited.

CHAPTER FIVE

JORGE

Fifteen years old

The chandeliers of the dining hall glowed with the flickering light of glass crystals that caught and scattered the golden hues of the two suns. My tray was balanced carefully in my hands, each step measured as I moved from one fairy dignitary to the next, refilling goblets and clearing empty plates.

I kept my head down, as I always did. It was safer that way. With Olric and Dain long gone, I'd been able to breathe easier these last three years. I could sleep without one eye open, my body braced for their next cruel prank.

The fairies barely noticed me—a human in their midst was as unremarkable as the tarnished cutlery they used to adorn their gilded table. And yet as I set a plate in front of one of the guests, I caught sight of a faint stain on its edge—a dull smear marring the sheen of the supposed gold.

It wasn't real gold. It was just an alloy. Evergrove Manor had sold off all its gold years ago, after King Oriven had died. Queen Indira's expenses had gone unchecked, and they were tendrils away from bankruptcy these days.

She might have driven her people to ruin entirely if not for a twist of fate. Another kingdom's chamberlain had stumbled upon my designs for pegasus shoes while at a dinner party. Word had spread quickly, and soon, other noble houses were bringing their steeds to me, eager for the innovative shoes that eased the strain on their wings and hooves. It wasn't long before an inventor took notice. He came, examined my work, and asked to buy the design.

Queen Indira hadn't hesitated. She sold the rights immediately. I was her servant, after all. I'd given the inventor everything he needed, knowing it would keep food on the table. That was all that mattered.

But the inventor had seen more than just the shoes. He caught sight of my carrier apparatus, the lightweight framework designed to redistribute cargo weight for pegasuses, allowing them to fly longer distances without injury. He'd purchased that design, too. The money had flooded in, enough to keep the manor from collapsing under its own excess.

That had been years ago. And now those funds were gone as well.

Queen Indira sat the head of the table. Her posture was poised and regal, her hands folded elegantly in her lap, her pale lavender skin glowing faintly in the dim light. She didn't look at me, didn't acknowledge my existence or my contribution.

My fingers brushed the edge of her plate as I refilled her glass. The metal responded, warming beneath my touch. I felt it yield to me, its surface softening, the tarnish dissolving like smoke. When I lifted my hand, the plate gleamed as though it had just been forged.

"I hear he's a terror on the battlefield." The thin-lipped noble with a nose perpetually tilted upward spoke with the air of someone who had never seen a battle but enjoyed discussing them over fine wine.

"They say the trolls scatter at the sight of him." This came from a broad-shouldered man draped in embroidered silks, his voice thick with self-importance.

"As well they should," Queen Indira chimed in. "He's the only thing keeping the Northern Border secure."

"Such a shame to think of a creature as lovely as our Princess Charlotte being sacrificed to a monster," said Thin Lips. "But that's royalty for you."

Their laughter was soft, almost pitying, as though they truly believed their sympathy carried weight. I glanced toward Charlotte at the far end of the table. She sat stiffly, her posture perfect, her gaze blank save for the faint curve of her lips—a mask of politeness she wore as easily as her silk gown.

But I knew better.

Her hands were hidden beneath the table. She wasn't paying attention to the conversation at all. She was watching the Convergence Games on her handheld crystal viewer.

A smirk tugged at my lips despite myself. That was Charlotte—silent rebellion wrapped in royal decorum. They all saw her as a perfect little princess, poised and obedient, ready to be bartered away for the good of the realm.

But I saw her—the real her. I saw the way her thumb slid over the edge of the crystal. I saw her eyes narrowing slightly as something on the screen caught her attention. Likely, Kael had delivered a devastating kick with his newly armored thighs. After the last games, Charlotte had come around to mechanical enhancements after Drakos had decimated the field with his fists of steel.

I turned back to my work, the tray feeling heavier in my hands now. The mention of the Beast Prince had tightened something in my chest, a knot of helpless anger that refused to ease. They talked about Charlotte's future as though she weren't sitting right there, as though she weren't a person with her own mind, her own will.

I stopped behind Charlotte's chair, wanting to offer her comfort in any way I could. She didn't look at me as I set her plate in front of her, didn't acknowledge my presence. She never did when others were watching. In Evergrove, it was unthinkable for a fairy princess to befriend a human servant.

Her fingers shifted slightly, angling the crystal viewer in her lap just enough for me to catch the glowing image on its surface so I could see her favorite champion at work. I personally thought Kael Drakos was a brute. I kept that opinion to myself.

"Charlotte, Lord Falcos wished you a happy birthday." Queen Indira's voice cut through the air like a blade.

Charlotte's head snapped up. The crystal fell from her hands. It hit the floor with a sharp crack. Silence hung heavy in the air, all eyes turning toward the princess and the glittering fragments of light at her feet.

Queen Indira's gaze darkened, her lips thinning into a line of icy displeasure. "What was that?"

"It was my fault, Your Highness." I stepped forward, lowering my tray and bowing my head.

The queen's sharp eyes fixed on me. I felt the weight of her stare like a physical blow.

"I was watching the Games. The crystal slipped from my hands."

A murmur rippled through the guests, their gazes shifting between me and the queen.

The thin-lipped man arched a brow. "Interesting. I wasn't aware the House of Evergrove paid its servants well enough to purchase a handheld crystal. And a human servant, no less."

"This one will not be an employee any longer." The Fairy Queen rose from her seat with a flourish. "You have disgraced this household. Leave. Now."

"Yes, Your Highness." I bowed my head lower, my body aching under the strain of my own unworthiness.

I took a step toward the door, but my foot landed wrong. The fragile bones in my ankle twisted. Pain shot up my leg. Before I could stop myself, my knees buckled. I crumpled to the ground in a graceless heap.

There were snickers from the highborn, low groans from the serving class. But all I heard was the sharp intake of breath that came from behind me. Charlotte rose so fast her chair scraped against the floor.

I gave a sharp shake of my head, warning her without words. She couldn't come near me. Not now. Not when all eyes were on us. Not when her mother's wrath was so dangerously close to turning on her.

Charlotte ignored me.

Bending slowly, deliberately, she picked up the fork she'd dropped onto the floor. She let out a long, low sigh. The sweetness of her breath tickled my nostrils. Like any taste of her I could get, I swallowed the scent down. She didn't look at me as she rose, her movements stiff and composed, and returned to her seat.

"Thank you for the birthday wishes, Lord Falcos. Thank you all for coming to my birthday party on this sacred night."

I pressed my palms against the cold, polished floor, forcing myself upright. My legs didn't tremble as I did. I felt nothing, not an ache or pain. The queen's attention was off me and back on her guests. Not only had I been dismissed, I was already forgotten.

The walk back to the stables felt longer than usual, the sounds of the party fading into the distance as the cool night air wrapped around me. Above, the sky was a swirling canvas of celestial light and shadow. The First Moon loomed high above, caught in the throes of the Hunter's Eclipse. The planet's shadow crept slowly across its surface, veiling its usual brilliance in a deep, blood-like crimson. The sight sent a chill through me, a reminder of how small I was beneath the weight of the cosmos.

I wasn't worried about being dismissed. I'd never received wages, just food and lodging. The queen couldn't afford to lose me—not when I was the one who cared for the animals. With the coffers bare, the queen still needed me to maintain the illusion of wealth with my forgery of metals and repairs of her tarnished trinkets.

The stables were quiet. The soft huffs of the pegasuses and the faint rustle of hay were the only sounds to greet me. I made my way over to the straw mattress. At least I'd get in some early rest and got out of cleanup duty.

I was awakened some time later by the soft creak of the stable door opening. Charlotte slipped through the gap, her cloak drawn tightly around her. She crossed to me in a few quick steps, her bare feet hardly making a sound on the dirt floor. When she reached me, she knelt, her blue eyes shimmering in the faint light.

"Let me see," she demanded, pulling at the threadbare sheet. She'd snuck in a thicker blanket years ago, but I kept it hidden and up high unless she was with me. When she was, I'd tuck her into its warmth.

"Charlotte, I'm fine."

Before I could stop her, she reached down and tore the covers away. The cool night air prickled against my skin, highlighting every imperfection. My legs were bent awkwardly, pale and too thin beneath the rough fabric of my trousers. There were reddish roses blooming on my knees where they'd slammed into the floor earlier, angry bruises spreading like ink beneath my skin. Along my shins, faint red marks traced where the forge fires had kissed too close during my work. A network of scars ran over my ankles, faint and silver from the strain of walking, running, existing in a world that was too heavy for me.

I couldn't feel a thing, not with her floral magic still caught in my nose and on the tip of my tongue.

She didn't say anything at first, just knelt beside me, her lavender fingers trailing over my battered knees. Her touch was feather-light, almost reverent, as if she feared breaking me further. The sight of her inspecting my weaknesses like it was her right to do so made my stomach twist. I turned my head away, swallowing down the shame.

"I wanted to apologize," she said.

"You never need to apologize to me."

"You always get in trouble because of me. And I just… I never — I'm a bad friend. You take the blame for me, you protect me, and I—" Charlotte shook her head. "It's never the other way around."

"I would never let you take a punishment for me. That's what friends are for."

She looked at me then, her eyes searching mine as though trying to find the truth in my words. I held her gaze. Neither of us spoke. Then she slipped closer and settled beside me on the straw mattress, but not before pulling the thicker blanket down from its high perch.

I couldn't feel any pain, not after she'd sighed her magic into me back in the dining hall. It was only my pain receptors that were muted. Charlotte's body next to mine set off pings of pleasure in every part of me.

"Do you want to hear who won the match?"

I nodded, leaning back against the wall as she began to speak. She rested her head on my chest. It was something she'd started doing last year when she'd first begun sneaking into the stables and lying next to me in the middle of the night.

I ran my fingers through her hair, braiding and unbraiding it. Which was another thing she'd told me she liked. Not so much my braiding designs, which she always unraveled because they were—in her opinion— awful. What she liked was the feel of my fingers in her hair.

Charlotte's voice washed over me like a gentle tide, each word soothing, even if I wasn't really listening. I caught fragments—the match was close, the final blow was devastating, her favorite champion had won—but most of it blurred together into a comforting hum. I closed my eyes, letting the sound of her voice ground me more than anything else in this world could.

She shifted closer, her arm brushing mine. My eyes opened. I turned my head to find her watching me. Her blue eyes were soft but intense.

"We're running out of time. We only have two more moons."

I didn't know what she was talking about. I was too fixated on her lips. They were a paler purple than the rest of her skin. I didn't know the name of the color.

"Jorge?"

She leaned in, her face so close now that I felt her breath against my cheek. My heart raced, a wild, uneven thing in my chest. She couldn't be about to—

I stopped her, my hand coming up to gently touch her shoulder. "You can't."

"You don't want me to kiss you?"

"Of course not."

"Of course not?" Charlotte reared back, putting an arm's length of distance between us.

"Charlotte, you know I'd give you anything, but—"

"It's my birthday. You haven't given me a present yet. And this is what I want."

"A kiss? From me?"

She nodded curtly. No, not curtly, courtly. It was the nod of a noble who expected their will to be followed without question.

"We can't."

"Is it because of the eclipse? Because tonight is the Hunter's Moon?"

On Lunaterra, it was sacrilege to share intimacies under any celestial event unless the couple were making a vow—a promise of forever. The gods were said to watch closely on nights like this, their judgment swift and merciless.

"You can't kiss me any day or night, Charlotte. The moons would damn me. Your mother would have me killed."

"No one will kill you," she snarled like a feral creature. "You are mine—You are my... you're my best friend."

"That's right." I ran my fingers through her hair, unraveling the braid I'd done for her. "I'm yours."

Charlotte's anger melted into something softer. Still feral, but with more presence of mind. "I don't want to marry him, Jorge. I don't want to be a sacrifice. I want... I want to go and see the games. Would you come with me?"

"Me?"

"Of course you. You promised you'd never leave me."

She was everything I wanted—everything I would never have. None of that mattered. I would give her anything. I would be anything. I would sacrifice everything just to see her happy.

"Of course I'll go with you. I'll follow wherever you lead."

It happened so fast there was nothing I could do. One moment, she was sitting an arm's distance away, her fists clenched and her eyes fierce. The next, she launched herself at me. Her arms wrapped around my neck. Her lips crashed into mine.

She was soft petals. I was brittle bones. Together we were forged steel—unyielding, unbreakable, fire and desperation.

I felt the first rays of the returning moonlight shining in through the cracks of the stables. The Eclipse was ending. Avarix was watching. He would punish us both.

I couldn't find the strength to care. Not when the object of my every waking desire was this close to me. Not when her warmth sank into my weary bones.

I had said I wouldn't kiss her. Let Avarix try and pull me away from her now. I wouldn't go. Not unless Charlotte pulled away from me.

She did not. She deepened the kiss, and I opened my soul to her. My heart was already hers; my entire existence might as well follow too.

When she pulled back, her breath came in soft, uneven gasps. Her face was so close I could still feel the heat of her skin against mine. Her blue eyes searched mine, wide and unguarded.

"You're mine."

The weight of her words settled deep in my bones, down into the marrow and reworking the cartilage. I could've moved a mountain if she'd asked. That kiss had changed everything. The trajectory of my life had shifted, tilting irrevocably toward her.

CHAPTER SIX

CHARLOTTE

The forest whispered around me, alive with the murmurs of the night. The leaves above rustled like secretive voices. The occasional chirp of nocturnal insects was interrupted by the sharp crack of a twig in the distance. Slick with sweat, my palms pressed against the rough bark of the tree I hid behind as a faint light pierced the darkness.

I crouched lower. The hem of my cloak skimmed the forest floor, catching on roots and damp leaves. The soft glow grew stronger. Lanterns swayed as a carriage rolled into view. Its light cut swaths through the deep shadows. My eyes landed on the sigil emblazoned on the carriage door—a blazing sun cradled by a crescent moon.

It was his emblem: Kael Drakos. The champion of the Sun and Moon Gauntlet.

For years, I had sat transfixed before a crystal viewer, watching Kael overcome every trial, outwit every opponent, and emerge victorious where so many fell. He was a force of nature. A legend. A symbol of resilience and triumph. And now, impossibly, he was here, not as a flickering image on a crystal screen but flesh and blood.

"Why are we stopping here?" Kael's voice was sharp, impatient, and entirely at odds with the steady, commanding presence I had imagined. He stumbled as he stepped down from the carriage, his footing unsteady. "Do you plan to have me stumble in the dark like some common fool?"

One of the servants, a thin, hunched man with trembling hands, scrambled to light another lantern. Kael's gaze landed on him like a predator zeroing in on wounded prey. The servant murmured an apology, his voice barely audible over the rustling leaves.

"Useless." Kael scoffed, the sound heavy with contempt. He took an unsteady step forward, his movements lacking the grace I had come to associate with him. "Get out of my sight before I decide you're not worth feeding tonight."

The servant scurried away, his head bowed. Kael turned toward another servant, who was adjusting the harnesses on the unicorns. Their shimmering horns were dimmed, their coats dull and dusky as though someone had stripped away their magic. Their heads hung low, their movements sluggish, a far cry from the vibrant, untamable creatures I had seen depicted in paintings.

Unicorns were prized for their speed, their hooves barely touching the ground as they streaked across open fields like shooting stars. But these creatures bore none of that legendary swiftness. Their legs trembled with each step, as though one more burden might send them to their knees. Their ribs pressed sharply against their hides, their once-proud manes tangled and limp. Someone had driven them too hard, drained them of their spirit. Another mile, another step, and they might stumble, too broken to rise again.

"If you take any longer, I'll harness you instead."

The servant flinched but worked quicker, his hands fumbling as Kael swayed slightly where he stood.

Was he drunk? This wasn't the champion who had faced down fire and shadow with unwavering determination. This wasn't the hero I had cheered for in the Games.

I took a step back, the movement small but enough to rustle the leaves beneath my foot. My heart lurched as the sound echoed louder than it should have, cutting through the night like a scream. Something cold and sharp pressed against my back.

"Step forward," a voice hissed in my ear.

I obeyed, my pulse pounding as I moved out of the shadows and into the faint glow of the lanterns. The champion's gaze snapped to me immediately, his dark eyes narrowing in suspicion.

"Who's this?" Kael demanded, his hand moving to the hilt of his sword.

My captor didn't answer. Their grip on me firmed as they pushed me farther into the light. The weight of Kael's stare was heavy, and… wrong. It felt like his eyes were roaming my body, particularly my breasts.

"Speak," the champion barked. "Who are you?"

I couldn't give him my name. Maybe just a piece of it. "My name is Char, and I'm a huge fan."

Kael's gaze swept over me, slow and deliberate, like a wolf sizing up a meal. My skin crawled under his attention, every inch of me wanting to recoil, but I stood tall, refusing to give him the satisfaction of flinching. The strong smell of the alcohol on his breath turned my stomach.

"A bit young, but that doesn't bother me. You'll make a fine bed partner for the night."

My frown deepened, the bile rising in my throat now threatening to choke me. "You're married to Tyra Veyne. What would she think of this?"

"She's not going to know. She married me for my victories, which is the same reason you're sneaking out in the middle of the night, on the path of my journey into the capital. You're not the first groupie to do so."

His mechanical hand reached out with a grinding whir of poorly maintained gears. I sidestepped his attempt easily, the sluggish movement of his enhanced arm telegraphing his intentions well before he could reach me.

"Don't touch me."

"Hard-to-Get is my least favorite game. Don't be difficult."

"Difficult? Difficult is cheering about your triumphs and thinking you were someone worth looking up to. Difficult is finding out the man I admired is nothing more than a philandering disappointment. I really believed your love story."

To think that my favorite champion and my favorite singer might have been faking their relationship for the crystals. Could this day get any worse?

"Admired?" A slurred chuckle escaped his lips. "Oh, sweetheart, admiration doesn't win medals."

He lunged at me, his movements clumsy, the grace he'd displayed in the Games when he was younger and less mechanized utterly absent. I ducked under his arm with ease, the scent of sour wine and sweat trailing after him.

Kael swung at me again, his fists slow and wide, more a brawler's heavy swing than the calculated strikes of a champion. I bobbed and weaved, dodging each clumsy attempt. My feet danced across the uneven forest floor, while his were rooted with the heavy armor of his mechanized legs.

I knew all his moves. Had practiced them for years. Right now, I could execute them better than him.

"Do you even know how many children across Lunaterra idolize you? We've all spent hours watching you, pretending to be you, dreaming of standing where you stand. And this is how you act? Pathetic."

I'd watched him battle fire, ice, and warriors from every corner of Lunaterra. The man before me now wouldn't last five minutes in the Games. His balance was off, his strikes lazy, his speed dulled by the weight of too many drinks and too much metal.

"Is this what you've been reduced to? A drunk stumbling through the woods, trying to grope women? How do you even plan to compete this year?"

His face darkened at that, his pride clearly stung. I ducked another swing, my reflexes sharp compared to his sluggish attempts. Kael stumbled, his rock of a foot catching on a root. He swayed but managed to stay upright. Barely.

I caught his wrist with one hand and twisted. It was a move I'd seen him perform dozens of times in the gauntlet. And it worked. I heard the distinct sound of bone popping and gears snapping. The champion dropped like a stone.

The collective gasp of the caravan snapped through the night like a whip. Lanterns swung as the others turned toward us, their eyes wide with disbelief and horror.

"Now you've done it," the man who had captured me hissed. "You've cost us the victory."

I tightened my grip on the dagger, my breath quickening as I counted the figures advancing on me. Their shadows stretched long and menacing in the dim light, their footsteps heavy and deliberate.

My mind raced, weighing my options. I could run, but they'd catch me. I could fight, but I was outnumbered. Either way, I would have to come up with yet a new plan.

CHAPTER SEVEN

JORGE

Eighteen years old

The ground was tough, dry, and reluctant to yield. I pressed on, driving the spade deep into the earth. My arms, no longer frail but lean with hard-won muscle, burned with the effort. It was a good burn, the kind that reminded me I was stronger now. My chest rose and fell steadily as I worked, each breath pushing me forward. My legs held firm beneath me, steady even after hours of standing, a far cry from the trembling weakness of my childhood.

I paused to wipe the sweat from my brow. The cool evening air brushed against my skin like a fleeting balm. The trench I'd dug stretched long and straight, ready to receive the seedlings. The nascent plants were hardy, stubborn things. They reminded me of myself—night-blooming varieties that could survive in barren soil and drink deeply of what little light the moon offered.

I crouched down, lowering the first seedling into the shallow trench with care. Its pale leaves caught what little light filtered down from Avarix. There were still faint traces of red on the moon's surface from the passing of the Hunter's Eclipse, leaving the first moon not in his full strength.

Over the years, the soil had turned against us, growing less fertile with each passing season. Some whispered that Avarix had withdrawn his favor from Solmane. The troll wars had drained the land of its people and its vitality. There was constant recruitment into the army. Every able body was conscripted to fight. They hadn't looked twice at me when they'd come by, skinny and frail as I was, barely more than a shadow of a man.

With my work in the fields done, I forced myself to stand. My bones ached, not just from the day's labor but from the frailty that never seemed to fully leave me. Mine was a life of constant effort. Always enduring.

Inside the stables, the dim light from the lanterns made shadows dance along the wooden walls. I shrugged out of my shirt. Sweat stained the garment and clung to me like a second skin. Grabbing a cloth from the nearest hook, I set about the task of wiping myself down. My arms were lead as I dragged the rough fabric across my face, savoring the simple relief of cool air against my damp skin. Until the cloth was snatched from my hands.

Charlotte held the cloth out of reach with an amused smirk. Her blue eyes sparkled in the lantern light. Her wild curls framed her lavender skin like a halo of shadows and moonlight.

"I like you better this way. Sweaty. Dirty. Raw."

I raised a brow at her, wiping my forearm across my forehead instead. "You're a fairy, Charlotte. Dirt sings to you. It stinks on me."

"I love the way you smell."

Her hand went to my chest. My weak heart went full gallop, racing to get closer to its mistress. Her nails raked over my flesh as though she could wrap her hand around her possession. She placed her button nose between my pecs and inhaled.

"My Jorge." Her voice was a whisper of breath against the fine hairs on my chest. And then she kissed me there. My heart skipped a beat.

She always initiated these moments. I always let her.

Not because I didn't want her—gods, I wanted her —because I didn't feel worthy of her light. So I let her take from me.

She blazed a trail of kisses across my chest. Then up the column of my neck. The moment her lips met mine, the reins of my self-control snapped. Her permission unleashed something wild inside of me. I kissed her back, letting every ounce of emotion I held for her pour into the act. My hands moved to her waist, pulling her closer as I deepened the kiss. Her fingers tangled in my hair, and I lost myself in her completely.

For her, I would endure every pain, every trial. For her, I would give everything I had, knowing it would never be enough.

"Kiss me, Jorge," she demanded against my parted lips.

"Where would you like me to kiss you, starlight?"

Charlotte broke our lip lock and walked backwards. As she did so, she lifted her dress to reveal her shapely calves and those lush purple thighs that made my mouth water. By the time she was on the mattress, she was nude up to her belly —save the birthday blade I'd fashioned for her years ago.

My legs got a renewed charge as I stalked toward her. I put a knee on the mattress, my weight causing her hips to settle into the center of the bedding. She spread her thighs wider, showing me the nectar at her pink core. I licked my lips in anticipation as I pressed my other knee into the mattress. Charlotte let her knees fall open.

After our first kiss at fifteen, we'd lain on this mattress most nights kissing. Months passed, and we began exploring with our hands. Mostly, she guided my hands where she wanted to be touched. Always, I followed her every command, cupping a breast, palming her ass. Then she sent me to her core.

One night, Charlotte woke in my arms to find me licking at my fingers. She'd been letting me put them inside her for a couple of weeks. At first, I'd fumbled to help her reach her ecstasy. It was long, patient work that I happily took on, eager for it to last an hour or more.

I'd discovered there were two spots at her core that would leave her body trembling and her wings fluttering. The first spot, a button at the apex of her treasure, made her quake with pleasure if I suckled at it for long moments. The second spot, buried inside her behind that nub, made her gush when I persistently pressed it.

I'd been trying to hide my perversion of lapping up her juices after she dozed in my arms. That night she'd caught me indulging. Instead of shaming me, which Charlotte never did, she spread her thighs and offered me access straight from the tap.

She'd been letting me kiss her between her thighs

ever since. I would happily spend hours drinking my fill of her nectar as she tried to douse her cries of pleasure with a fist to her mouth, a pillow over her head, or even holding her breath. Each cry that escaped her perfect lips made me feel like the strongest man in the world.

Charlotte patted the mattress. "Lie down so I can sit on your face, Jorge."

"If that would please Your Highness."

Her grin spread impossibly wide as I did as I was told. I lay on my back and pulled her over top of me, taking care to avoid the blade that was always strapped to her thigh. I pressed the tip of my tongue to her bud. Charlotte let out a low moan.

"Hush or they'll hear you."

"I don't care," she sighed, palming her breasts.

"If they hear how I please you, they'll take me from you."

"Never. No one will ever take you from me. You're mine."

It was a game she liked to play. The notion of being found out heightened her pleasure. Not that we ever had been found out. Her mother was often away attending parties or having affairs with young male fae. Charlotte always came late at night when the house was in slumber. She'd sneak back to her bed before Solara rose in the morning, then stayed in bed until long after Lyra was following her mother across the sky in the afternoons.

No one suspected anything of this fairy princess who didn't rise before dawn. No one suspected she sought pleasure in the human weakling that slept in the stables.

Despite my teasing, Charlotte climaxed quickly. I knew every flick of tongue to get her where she wanted to be, which was writhing over me. When her hips began to buck and her wings broke free of her dress, I kept my tongue working, this time deeper inside her core. It drew out the pleasure, ensuring that her next climax would be deeper and longer. It meant I could take my time and suckle every petal of her folds as she dripped that sweet nectar directly into my mouth, smeared it on my face, and left her imprint on my soul.

The stable door creaked open.

The sound was a shard of ice through the haze of our shared heat. I froze, my body stiffening as light spilled into the stables. Charlotte pulled away, her eyes wide with alarm as we both scrambled to sit up. My legs protested the sudden movement, nearly giving out beneath me as I stumbled off the straw mattress.

A woman stood in the doorway, her figure backlit by the faint glow of the moons. Her dark robes billowed around her. The garment was embroidered with shimmering constellations that shifted as she moved. A silver sigil glinted on her chest, marking her as a Sky Keeper Mage, one of the powerful envoys entrusted with maintaining the celestial balance of Lunaterra.

Her sharp eyes, the color of storm clouds, swept over the stables. They landed on us with an expression that was all disdain and no shock. Her lips curled as if she had already judged us unworthy.

"Well, well. What do we have here?"

The mage stopped at the nearest stall, leading her pegasus into the area. Its wings, speckled with the colors of twilight, quivered as she guided it inside and secured its reins with a flick of her fingers. The creature settled, though its luminous eyes stayed fixed on me, almost accusing.

"The queen will not like this," said the mage, her voice cool and measured.

"My mother isn't here."

"I meant the Lioness Queen, Your Highness. Though your fiancé occasionally slacks his lusts, it is uncomely for the bride to do so. Personally, I think that a double standard."

I didn't know much about the Sky Keeper Mages of Solmane. They were not like the priests and holy men of other nations and religions who swore off women. Sky Keeper Mages took their pleasure but made no commitments.

Charlotte stepped forward, her shoulders squared and her chin lifted in defiance. "You will say nothing of this."

"Unlike your stable toy, I don't work here, Your Highness. Your orders mean nothing to me. I come to check on the future queen's… progress."

"Then take your report back to the Lioness Queen and the Beast Prince Adom that I am advanced in all my studies and await the appointed time of our nuptials at the next Hunter's Eclipse."

Charlotte moved in front of me. It's what she always did whenever there was a hint of the two of us being found out. She put her glowing self on display so that others would forget my presence. It wasn't working this time.

"Forgive me, Highness, but for some reason I doubt that you will show up for your appointed nuptials on time. I get the sense that you might lose your way to the capital."

Charlotte's body went taut like a bowstring. Her hand clenched into a fist at her side. Then slowly, deliberately, her fingers uncurled. When they did, the blade was in her grasp, gleaming with a cold, deadly light.

"You're right," she said, her voice the polite fairy princess' who was all manners and decorum. "I won't make it to my wedding. I've made other plans for that day."

Before I could fully register what was happening, Charlotte moved. A blur of lavender skin and shimmering wings, she lunged at the Sky Keeper Mage, flipping the dagger in her hand and striking with the hilt instead of the blade. The move was so quick, so precise, it was over before I even had time to react.

The mage staggered. Her staff clattered to the ground as her eyes rolled back. She crumpled in a heap at Charlotte's feet.

I blinked, my mouth opening to say something—anything—but no words came.

Charlotte's fiery gaze snapped to me, her breath coming fast, as though the act of violence had ignited something within her. She knelt, slipping on her shoes with a speed born of urgency, and grabbed my hand.

"It's time. We're running."

I should've hesitated. I should've thought of a better strategy—like not running on foot with my weak body, which would inevitably fail me. Or something like saddling the strongest pegasus in the stables and flying out of Evergrove. Because make no mistake, I had every intention of following Charlotte wherever she went, or wherever she was taken.

Where I was calm and logic, Charlotte was all fire and instinct. We raced toward the stable doors instead of the stalls. Every rational thought in me screamed that this was a terrible idea, but my mind, my body, my entire being was so used to following her that that's exactly what I did. I followed my wild fairy princess right into the open arms of danger.

Charlotte threw open the doors, and we came face to face with a dozen soldiers. Their polished armor glinted in the light of the First Moon, their swords drawn and ready. Charlotte did not let go of my hand, not even as the soldiers reached for us and tore us apart.

"Don't touch him! He is mine! You let him go this instant!"

"That's enough, Charlotte." Queen Indira stood a few paces away. Her gaze swept over us, her expression one of thinly veiled disgust. "I thought you'd be over this childhood dalliance by now."

She knew. She'd known. My knees threatened to give out, but I held firm. Mainly because I was being held by soldiers with muscles bigger than my head.

Charlotte's demeanor shifted so fast it felt like a physical blow. Her face blanked into the cool, imperious mask of royalty. She tilted her chin, her gaze hardening as she looked down her nose at me.

"I was just practicing with him, Mother." Her voice

was cold, each word clipped and perfect. "I didn't want to go to Prince Adom inexperienced, as I know how worldly he is. I wanted to ensure I was the perfect wife in all ways. The human was convenient. He keeps his mouth shut and does as he's told. I'm done with him now."

I knew, deep down, there wasn't a parsec of truth in her words. They grated because they should've been true. A fairy princess shouldn't care for a human stable boy.

Queen Indira's lips curved into a matronly smile. It sent a chill down my spine because she'd never done a maternal thing in all the years I'd been here. "Excellent. Now that you're done with him, I'll discard him for you."

Charlotte's mask cracked, a fine fissure above her brow as her fingers curled at her sides. "You're going to fire him? We do still have need of him."

"No, I'm not going to fire him. I'm going to send him to the Convergence Games the two of you love to watch so much."

"The Games?" Charlotte's mask shattered entirely.

She didn't need to say anything else. I was stronger, due to all the jobs I'd taken on around the failing manor. But we both knew I wouldn't survive five minutes in the Games. I was barely able to hold my own against the rigors of stable work and all my added duties, let alone face warriors and beasts bred for bloodshed.

"He'll be fodder for the games. A fitting end for a human who dared to overstep."

Charlotte dropped all pretense. She lunged forward, her hand reaching for mine. Her grip was fierce, desperate, as though her touch alone could anchor me to safety. "No. You can't. I won't let you."

The guards moved between us, their armor clanking as they wrenched us apart. Charlotte did not let go of my hand. So I held on to hers.

"I'll survive, Charlotte. And then I'll find you."

I knew there was no way we'd come out of this night together, but I would get back to her. If they sent me to the games, I'd kill anyone, anything, to claw my way back to her. If I was killed, I'd become a ghost and haunt the halls of wherever she lived. As long as she wanted me, I would always find my way to her.

I didn't register the pain immediately. Not until I saw her hand jerk away from mine. And then my hand fell from my body.

Charlotte screamed, a sound so raw it echoed in my skull. I looked down, and for a brief, disoriented moment, I didn't understand what I was seeing.

My hand—my hand was no longer attached to my arm.

The pain came then, sharp and blinding. It ripped

through every nerve in my body. I heard Charlotte cry out again. Her voice broke into sobs. And then the world tilted.

The stables, the guards, even the stars above, blurred into nothingness. And then everything went black.

CHAPTER EIGHT

CHARLOTTE

I woke with a start, my head pounding, the taste of copper in my mouth. Blinking hard, I sat up and took in my surroundings. A single lantern hung from a crooked beam, casting flickering light over the bare stone walls. The floor was rough beneath me, scattered with straw that smelled of bodily fluids. Wooden bunks lined one side of the room, their mattresses little more than sagging heaps of cloth.

I knew this place. The low, oppressive ceiling, the cracked stone, the faint hum of wards in the air—I'd seen it before. On the crystals.

This was the warrior room of the Convergence Games tournament. Specifically, the fresh meat quarters. These were the rooms for those who had been thrown into the Games without a prayer of surviving. A place for bodies meant to fall in the first round, to sate the crowd's bloodlust before the real competitors took the stage.

Jorge had been here.

Three years ago, I'd watched him fight on the same crystal viewer I'd once held between us. I'd seen the dirt on his face in my pristine screen. The weakness in his body as he struggled against opponents who outmatched him in strength and ferocity.

He hadn't died.

But he hadn't won, either.

He'd simply disappeared.

I knew in my heart he still lived. Because my heart still beat. The moment his stopped, mine would too.

So he had to be here somewhere. Or if not, someone knew where he'd gone or been taken to. If I could survive this—if I could endure the gauntlet of fire, shadow, and teeth that awaited me—maybe I'd find out what happened to him. Maybe I'd find him.

The thought steadied me, even as my surroundings pressed in on me. I pushed myself to my feet. My hand brushed the wall for support, the rough stone cold against my fingertips.

"First time?"

The voice came from one of the bunks. A woman, who could have been my mother's age, sat up. Her face was shadowed, her eyes sharp. She had the look of someone who'd been here too long, her hair matted, her posture wary.

"Yes," I said, my voice steady despite the nerves clawing at my throat.

She snorted softly, shaking her head. "Doesn't matter how many times you come through here. It's always the same. Fear. Blood. Death."

"How many times have you been here?"

She shrugged. "This will be my fourth game."

Four games? That meant twelve years. "If you survive, they keep you here? In these quarters?"

I began searching the shadows, looking for his dark hair and kind eyes.

"Unless you win." She snorted again, as though someone like her winning was a joke. "If you choose to stay, it's not a bad life. You get to live the years between the games fed, housed. But you have to survive first."

As though to punctuate her words, a gong sounded. The vibrations shook the stone walls and made my teeth ache.

"You said choose? What's the other choice?"

The woman ignored my question. Her shoulders

stiffened as she walked away, leaving me with the words echoing in my mind: *You have to survive first.*

The gong reverberated again, louder this time, its sound heavy with finality. The fighters around me shifted uneasily, a murmur of fear and tension rippling through the group. Most gazes darted toward the heavy iron gates that loomed ahead. A few, however, stood calm and still, their eyes cold and calculating. Veterans, no doubt. Survivors of past games. I wondered how many of them had started in the Fresh Meat brigade like me, how many had clawed their way out, only to return to this blood-soaked arena.

The gates groaned as they began to lift, the sound grating and slow. Beyond them, the arena stretched wide and ominous. Avarix hung heavy in the sky, his pale glow dimmed as he prepared to be eclipsed in a couple of days' time.

Three years ago, Jorge had been here. He had walked these halls, slept in these quarters, fought in these games. He had survived. And then he'd disappeared. And he hadn't come back for me. I had to believe the reason was that he couldn't.

Just as I'd felt his pain when they took his hand, and the pain when he was hurt in these games, I was going to make them hurt. Then I was going to make them tell me where he was.

The roar of the crowd hit me like a wall, a deafening

wave that vibrated through my chest and threatened to unsteady my legs. I stepped forward into the light, my boots sinking slightly into the loose, packed dirt of the coliseum floor. It was overwhelming—too loud, too bright, too real.

The Sun and Moon Gauntlet was a spectacle of strategy and survival. I'd watched it from the safety of soft cushions and flickering light, cheering for my favorites, marveling at their strength. Standing in the middle of it as part of the Fresh Meat brigade, it didn't feel anything like I'd imagined.

The coliseum stretched endlessly. Its towering walls of stone blotted out the horizon. High above, the crowd loomed like a living, shifting sea. Their cheers and jeers merged into a chaotic symphony of expectation.

I focused on the ground, on the faint pattern of marks etched into the dirt where countless others had stood before me. My heart raced, each beat loud and insistent in my ears, but I forced myself to breathe.

The announcer's voice boomed over the chaos, a sharp, clipped tone that echoed against the coliseum walls. "And now, the Fresh Meat! Witness their struggle, their desperation, their fight to survive!"

On one of the massive crystals embedded in the coliseum's walls, I saw myself. A girl with tangled curls, lavender skin smudged with dirt, and a defiant tilt to her chin. She looked braver than I felt. Her blue eyes were steady despite the chaos around her.

I could do this. I had to do this.

Across the arena, a massive gate creaked open, revealing the first challenge. A surge of heat rolled out from the gate, accompanied by the crackling sound of fire. The first section of the gauntlet—solar flames danced along the ground, forming shifting paths of fire that burned hotter than the forge back home. The forge that had remained cold after Jorge's abduction.

The Sun and Moon Gauntlet had begun. My body moved on instinct, dodging and weaving through the searing paths. The fire roared, hungry and alive. The heat scorched the air around me, leaving my throat dry and raw. I kept my eyes on the ground, focusing on the flicker of flames and the safe spaces between them.

The crowd roared again, their voices a distant blur as my world narrowed to the challenge in front of me. The fire was relentless, shifting, and unpredictable. I stayed light on my feet, my training kicking in as I moved with purpose. I knew these games. I knew how to win.

The fire lunged toward me like a living beast, but I was faster. I leapt through the final gap, the heat licking at my heels, and landed hard on the other side. My heart thundered in my chest, every muscle coiled tight as I took a steadying breath.

The scent of charred air filled my lungs. I barely registered it. I was already looking ahead—to the next barrier, to the next fight. No time to rest, no time to falter.

A sharp scream split the air behind me. I turned just in time to see another contender caught in the flames. It was the woman who'd been here four times. This was her last.

The crowd cheered, indifferent to the life snuffed out before them. If I were back home with a crystal viewer in my hand, I doubt I would've registered her death.

I clenched my fists. There was no room for hesitation, no space for mercy. I lifted my chin, stepped forward, and faced the next trial.

CHAPTER NINE

JORGE

Twenty-One

"**W**as this the best idea, Your Highness? There are reports of trolls in the woods."

The waiting room of the summer castle was stifling, its grandeur only amplifying the weight in my chest. The stone walls were draped with rich tapestries that muted the echoes of my pacing, while the faint scent of polished wood and beeswax lingered in the air. The

Hunter's Eclipse was only two days away, its pull a constant reminder of what was coming.

"Much rather fight a troll than..." Prince Adom trailed off, but I knew the trajectory of his thoughts.

"Than face your bride?"

The first time I'd seen the Prince of Solmane, I'd thought him a nightmare come to life. Half lion, half man, his form a monstrous blend of power and fury, a predator on two legs. He'd looked like the kind of creature who'd devour a fairy princess whole. The kind of creature who would destroy Charlotte if he got his sharp claws on her.

I'd stayed awake in the barracks each night, my body aching from training, my hand blistered from wielding weapons too heavy for my frame. Pain I was used to. The surprising thing was how natural killing came to me.

They'd shoved my still bleeding body onto the battlefield after I'd barely survived the Convergence Games. They put a cheap prosthetic hand that ended in a sword at the end of my arm and aimed me at a troll. I didn't think. I just swung.

My blade tore through the air, heavy with the weight of every injustice I'd ever endured—being born weak, growing up without parents, suffering under my uncle's fists and against my cousins' kicks. I struck with the fury of every scar carved into my skin, not caring if it broke the brittle bones inside me.

I didn't break. The troll did. I poured everything into that blow—a reckoning, a demand, a promise. I would never be powerless again.

Battle had a way of changing a man. I fought my way up from a conscript to a soldier, from a soldier to a commander, my body reforged in the crucible of war. Every commendation, every victory came with enhancements—first a crude mech arm to replace the one I lost, then the reinforced plating in my legs that let me run faster, strike harder, survive longer. The weak, frail servant who had once been unable to protect Charlotte was gone. In his place was something sharper, something deadlier. A weapon honed for vengeance.

And with every battle, every rise in rank, I found myself closer to the Beast Prince. Close enough to see him, to know him. Close enough to kill him. Close enough right now that the blade embedded in my prosthetic would gut him and leave him to bleed out slowly while we waited for Charlotte's arrival two days before her wedding.

I stared down at my fake hand. "No wonder this first date feels more like an ambush than anything."

"Don't be fooled," growled Prince Adom. His growl wasn't one of anger. It was simply his normal tone of voice. "Royalty are the stealthiest and most cunning fighters in the world."

I snorted at that. "I hear she's beautiful."

"It's a marriage of convenience. Her looks don't matter. There will be no courtship. No love. I'm doing my duty—to the moon, to my people, and to end this war."

I put my hand at my back. The lethal blade remained inside its sheath. "Good for you, Highness. Love gets people killed."

The Beast Prince had no interest in loving Charlotte. His only joy came from slaughtering trolls. I'd seen him cleave through the enemy like wheat in the fields, his roar shaking the earth as he defended the lands of Solmane. He had no interest in glory. He never expected his people to love him. Didn't expect his bride to care for him.

He'd never even tried to meet the Princess of Evergrove, let alone win her over. If anything, he seemed content to keep the union and any knowledge of his bride-to-be at arm's length.

That disinterest caused my guard to slip. It gave me time to see behind his beastly exterior. To get to know the man beneath. In a short time, I came to respect the Prince of Solmane. Then grudgingly to call him a friend.

And yet friendship wasn't enough to stop what I was going to do to him today.

"You're going to terrify the poor girl."

"Precisely. I want her to see me, get her screams out of the way, and then move on to the wedded bliss portion of our lives together where we rarely see or speak to each other."

I flexed my mechanical hand, the faint hum of its joints a constant reminder of what I'd lost—and what I'd built in its place. The original mech arm they'd slapped on me after I'd made it out of the Games and had been conscripted into the army had been a clunky amalgamation of steel and wires that barely functioned. It had been heavier than my entire arm used to be, making every movement feel like I was dragging an anchor.

Over the years, I'd spent every spare moment refining it. Every bit of pay I earned from the army went toward materials and tools. The original steel was replaced with a lightweight alloy I forged myself, one that didn't buckle under strain or chafe against my skin. The clunky gears were swapped for streamlined mechanisms, each piece calibrated for precision.

The door creaked open, and Adom roared. A quick check in my peripheral showed the Beast Prince with his maw shut, slinking deeper into the shadows as though they could grant him a few more minutes before he had to come face to face with his bride.

Adom hadn't roared. That was the sound of my pulse in my ears, drowning out everything but the unbearable anticipation coiling inside me. My fingers twitched at my side, one hand clenching into a fist, the other—phantom though it was—aching as if I could still feel the last thing it had ever touched.

Her hand.

For three years, I had lived in the echo of that moment, trapped in the memory of her fingers tangled with mine, her warmth grounding me right before they ripped us apart. In my mind, I was still holding her hand. I had never let go.

The scent of flowers wafted into the room before she stepped through the doors. It wasn't her usual fragrance. Not the warm, familiar blend of lavender and soft earth that had lingered in my memories for years. This was sharper, sweeter, like a bouquet arranged to impress rather than comfort. My nose twitched, my instincts prickling.

Maybe she'd changed. I was no longer the fragile boy I'd been when we'd met. My body bore the marks of every battle fought, my muscles carved from years of hardship and survival. Even as I told myself that people could change, something about that scent scratched at the back of my mind like an itch I couldn't reach.

"If you don't want to be queen, all you need to do is scream," I said, my voice low, testing.

She was veiled. Adorned in white. Her gown flowed like liquid moonlight. "Are you going to bite me now?"

The hairs on the back of my neck stood on end. That wasn't Charlotte's voice. "Remove the veil."

Her fingers curled into the fabric, clutching it tightly. "Human custom dictates it's bad luck to see the bride before the wedding day."

I knew her hands, every delicate line, every callus from years of secret work with tools and weapons. These hands were different. This wasn't my Charlotte. She might as well have been a troll.

The fury that I'd kept buried roared to life. I moved without thinking, my body a blur as I lunged forward to rip the veil away myself.

"Do not touch her."

Adom's hand shot out. Deadly claws clamped around my neck with a vise-like grip. The pressure was immediate, cutting into my air and sending a sharp pulse of pain down my spine.

"Something isn't right," I choked out, my voice strained as Adom's grip tightened.

My dark eyes darted past him to the veiled figure pressed against the door. Her back was flat against the wood as though she could vanish into it. Charlotte never cowered, not even the one time in her life she'd been scared.

This wasn't her—it couldn't be.

"Show yourself." I braced for her to run, ready to give chase if she did.

"It's bad luck to see the bride before the wedding. I was trying to honor your father's human customs, Your Highness."

Adom's gaze shifted from me to her. The change in his focus made him loosen his grip on my throat. I staggered back, dragging in a ragged breath as the room spun for a moment.

"Leave us," Adom said, his voice a cold command.

"Adom—"

"Now."

A thousand protests screamed in my mind. In the end, I obeyed, retreating from the room. My feet carried me to the garden, though my mind was already circling back to that door, to that veiled imposter. That wasn't her. It couldn't have been.

Could it?

I paced the garden like a caged animal, my thoughts tearing at me. Could Charlotte have changed so much in three years? Could she have forgotten me entirely?

My heart rebelled at the thought. Logic whispered cruel possibilities. She was a princess. I was nothing. Of course, she'd forgotten me.

But no. I refused to believe it. Not my Charlotte. In order for me to believe it, she'd have to tell me herself.

Movement caught my eye up the castle wall. The flicker of a figure in the window above me made my pulse spike. It was her. Or was it?

I didn't stop to think. My hands found purchase on the rough stone. I climbed, the muscles in my arms burning as I pulled myself upward.

The window creaked open as I swung myself over the ledge. My breath came in sharp bursts, but not from the climb. There she was—without the veil this time. Her hair had Charlotte's lavender hues, her skin the same soft tones. But the rest of her…

It was not the pert nose I'd memorized. That was not the slope of her shoulders. Those were not the wings I'd traced as she slept in my arms.

"I knew it wasn't you. Where is she?"

The imposter opened her mouth, but no words came out. Her lips trembled, caught between fear and a lie she couldn't summon fast enough.

Before I could demand an answer, a deafening roar shattered the silence. The walls shook with the force of it. Adom's hands yanked me backward, dragging me over the windowsill. My feet hit the ledge, and we both tumbled, gravity claiming us in a chaotic tangle of limbs and fury.

We hit the ground in a bone-jarring collision,

already throwing blows before the dust had time to rise. His claws tore at my armor, screeching against the metal as he searched for weakness. The air between us reeked of fury and sweat, punctuated by the sharp tang of his beastly growl.

"Adom, it's not what you think."

"I think you were trying to steal my bride."

"That's true. But not…*her*."

I twisted a gear in my prosthetic arm. With a sharp click, the mechanism disengaged his hold. His claws snapped back, leaving me space to breathe.

"Adom, listen to me. She's not—"

Another blow silenced me. This one drove the air from my lungs. I staggered but caught myself, my feet skidding on the dirt. Then the scent hit me: trolls.

Adom smelled it, too. His golden eyes flicked to the tree line. His snarl deepened, this time directed at the true threat. We broke apart, both turning to face the hulking figures emerging from the shadows.

The trolls charged with brutal speed. Adom leapt into action, his massive claws slicing through the air as he engaged two of them at once. Their heavy clubs swung wildly. The Beast Prince moved with the precision of a predator, each strike calculated to destroy.

I turned toward the third troll and froze. It wasn't coming for me. It was making a beeline for her—the veiled woman cowering near the wall. The imposter.

Even though I knew she wasn't Charlotte, she was still an innocent. I wouldn't let her die.

I bolted, my prosthetic arm whirring as I activated its blade. The troll swung its club. I ducked low, sliding beneath its blow and coming up with a slash that tore through its hamstring. It roared in pain. I didn't give it the chance to recover. My blade found its throat. With a final gurgling cry, it crumpled to the ground.

The woman stumbled into my arms, trembling. There was no pull, no familiar warmth that would've rooted me to the spot. Her scent was wrong—almost like Charlotte's, but not quite. A pale imitation. But there was enough of Charlotte's scent on her to confirm one thing: Charlotte had been with her.

Adom prowled toward us. I let her go, nudging her toward him. Once the prince had her, I slipped away before he could notice.

I backtracked to the carriage in the stables. The pegasuses were familiar, as was the carrying apparatus harnessed to their backs. Even their hooves were shoed with my design. For a brief second, I felt pride that my inventions had cared for Charlotte in my absence.

Charlotte. Where was she? The scent of her lingered.

I activated the scanner in my prosthetic, running it over the area. The faint glow illuminated a trail—her trail—leading to the wall.

She'd gone over it.

I scaled the stone barrier, my muscles burning with the effort. On the other side, the forest stretched out in darkness. I followed the tracks, the cold night air biting at my skin.

A few miles down the path, there were signs of a scuffle: broken branches, disturbed earth, wagon tracks cutting deep into the dirt. There was a concentration of her scent in a clearing. There had been a skirmish, by the looks of things. She'd been taken.

I followed the tracks of the carriage. Soon the forest thinned, giving way to open fields. Then the outskirts of the capital. The trail led me straight onto the bustling city streets. Here, amidst the noise and chaos, it vanished.

I pressed my palm against the city wall, letting the cool stone ground me as my thoughts spiraled. She was alive. I knew that much. If she'd died, I would've felt it, an ache that no amount of enhancements or strength could dull.

The crowd surged around me, the energy of the Games pulling them toward the coliseum. I let myself be carried along, my mind spinning with questions and doubts. And then I saw it.

A crystal screen mounted high on the side of a building, its surface shimmering with the broadcast of the Games. The roar of the crowd in the coliseum echoed through the streets. It was the fresh meat brigade. I remembered it all too well from the last game three years ago. It was a recurring nightmare. I almost looked away, but something inside warned me not to blink.

And there she was.

Charlotte.

Her lavender skin gleamed under the spotlight. Her violet hair cascaded down her back like silk. She stood tall, defiant, her blue eyes scanning the arena as if she were daring it to break her. Panic and fury collided in my chest, a storm of emotions that left me reeling.

She was in the Games. Of all the schemes I'd come up with over the last three years—of how to snatch Charlotte on the road to the castle, or the night before her wedding, or to sweep her away as she walked down the aisle—this had not been a consideration in my battle plans.

Charlotte was in the Games. How had she ended up here? It didn't matter. Whether I'd grab her from my best friend's claws or swoop her from the ravages of the games, it didn't matter. Now that I'd found her, I would get her back.

CHAPTER TEN

CHARLOTTE

After the introductions, we were led to another holding cell. This was yet another part of the games I didn't get to see on the crystals. What did surprise me was the sounds that carried from the arena and into the cell.

From beyond the barred gate, the muffled roar of the crowd reached us, swelling and falling like a tide being pulled by the strength of more than one moon. Beneath that were other sounds. These were the sickening thuds of flesh striking flesh. The sharp snap of bones breaking. The guttural cries of pain. These were the sounds of bodies being broken, of spirits being crushed as some fought to get out of the queue, while others were eager to get into the arena.

My ears strained to catch the announcer's voice cutting through the noise. It was drowned out by the desperate sobbing of a man crouched in the corner. His shoulders heaved with each shuddering breath, his face buried in his trembling hands. He wasn't alone. Some prayed in whispers, their words stumbling over each other like a lifeline they were clinging to. Others simply sat in numbed silence, staring ahead as though trying to accept their fate before it reached them.

No one here was rooting for anyone else. There were no alliances in this place. We were all competitors.

No, that's wrong. We were all prey. Each person clinging to whatever scraps of courage they could muster.

I tightened my grip on my dagger. Its weight felt heavier than it had when I trained with it in the safety of the Evergrove woods. My palms were damp, but my grip remained true. The leather Jorge had fashioned on the hilt was perfectly curved to my palm so it wouldn't easily slip from my grasp.

The door creaked open. A sliver of light spilled into the room. The beam was harsh and unkind, illuminating the raw terror etched on the faces around me. A guard barked something unintelligible. In response, we all lurched to our feet like puppets on strings, driven by survival instinct rather than the will to obey.

We were led back down the narrow corridor from which we'd entered. The sounds of the arena grew louder, more visceral. My steps faltered.

I forced myself to straighten, lifting my chin as we reached the final gate. Beyond it, the blinding light of the arena awaited a world of chaos and death disguised as entertainment. And now it was my turn.

Overhead, Avarix shone bright and cruel, his pale light casting long shadows across the vast coliseum floor. I'd watched these games my entire life, studied every move, memorized every strategy. Nothing could have prepared me for the raw, unrelenting reality of the arena.

The first barrier loomed ahead: a towering wall of fire. The flames roared and twisted, impossibly high and alive. Their searing heat reached me even at a distance. Sweat trickled down my back. The air shimmered, heavy and suffocating, and the acrid scent of burning filled my nose.

I crouched low, scanning the blaze. The Games were brutal, but they weren't chaos. They were a test of skill, precision, and timing. There was a pattern there. My eyes darted over the flames, following the rhythm of their flicker, the brief, tantalizing gaps that opened and closed like the teasing nip of a predator before its jaws swallowed you whole.

To my right, one of the other contenders surged forward, clearly thinking the same thing. He was broad-shouldered and muscled, his movements brash and confident as he charged toward the wall of fire without hesitation. But his timing was off—by just a fraction of a second.

The flames surged, hungry and unforgiving, engulfing him mid-stride. His scream tore through the air before being belched back up with a roar of the fire. The smell of charred flesh hit me, and I clenched my jaw to keep from retching.

I couldn't look away, even though every instinct screamed at me to move. The man collapsed. His scorched body crumpled to the ground—a puppet with its strings cut. He didn't get back up.

The crowd erupted in cheers, their bloodlust palpable even from here. I tore my gaze from the fallen contender and fixed it on the flames. The flicker, the shift, the gap—it was there, just waiting for the right moment. My muscles coiled as I tracked the rhythm, and when the opening appeared, I sprinted forward.

The heat slammed into me like a wall, a scorching wave that stole the breath from my lungs. The hairs on my arms were singed. The edges of my sleeves curled from the embers, catching them.

I dashed through. My boots thudded against the charred ground, the flames licking at my heels. I didn't falter. I made it through.

The air on the other side was cooler, thinner, though still tainted with the acrid scent of smoke and flesh. I stumbled to a stop, my chest heaving as I sucked in breath after desperate breath. My skin stung, raw from the heat, but I was alive. I glanced back at the wall of fire just as it roared again, sealing off the path behind me.

The second barrier rose before me: a twisting maze of spikes that shifted unpredictably. No, not unpredictably. Again, there was a pattern.

I darted forward, narrowly avoiding a spike that shot out beside me, then leapt over another that erupted from the ground. I'd seen this before in the games. I knew how to win. Though that knowledge and the actions didn't translate smoothly in real life.

I crouched low, my breath steadying as I mapped the movements with my eyes. One spike hissed upward, another swept sideways, and a third struck like a viper before pulling back into its hole. That was it. Much like a ballroom dance.

A step, a pause, a spin. The spikes moved in a predictable cadence, shifting in and out of the ground like partners waiting for their turn on the floor. I inhaled, centering myself, letting the pattern sink into my bones. Then I stepped onto the dance floor.

The first spike hissed upward at my side like an overeager partner reaching for my waist. I pivoted smoothly, allowing it to graze the air where I had been a breath before. Another blade swept low, cutting a deadly arc toward my ankles. I leapt, landing lightly as though twirling through a reel, my feet whispering across the uneven ground.

I dipped beneath the next spike, my body bending with the effortless grace of a practiced turn. The grinding metal around me was a chorus, the screech of shifting blades a twisted symphony to accompany my waltz.

A blade shot toward my ribs. I spun, allowing it to pass like a miscalculated step in a dance, my skirt fluttering as I avoided the killing blow. Another rose beneath me—I leapt, twisting midair, my arms flaring outward before my boots touched down in perfect form.

The crowd roared. I barely heard them. I had danced this dance before. Not with steel, but men who thought they could lead me. Same difference, really. And just like in those ballrooms, I was the one that was truly leading.

The music ended. The blades aimed away from me, awaiting their next partners. I'd made it. For now.

The third challenge wasn't a barrier at all. It was a face-off against the fighters who'd made it through in the last games.

Jorge had been in the last games. He'd made it past this level. And then he'd vanished from the screen. Would he reappear now? Would I face off against the man that I loved in a battle to the death? It was the only way I wanted to die, with his hands on any part of me, including my throat.

The first man to face me was not Jorge. His shoulders were broad and his arms augmented with gleaming prosthetics that hissed and whirred as he moved. His right arm ended in a blade, the edge wickedly curved. He didn't ask if I was ready as Jorge would have. He didn't wait for me to make the first move. He lunged for me.

I met him with my dagger, deflecting his blade and twisting away. His movements were sharp, efficient, mechanical in a way I could anticipate. I'd studied fighters like him. I knew their weaknesses.

What I hadn't prepared for was the second fighter.

A sharp kick sent me sprawling, my dagger skidding across the dirt. I rolled, narrowly avoiding a follow-up strike, and scrambled to my feet. The second fighter was leaner, faster, her prosthetic legs propelling her forward with terrifying speed. She grinned, her teeth flashing in the spotlight, as if she already knew I was done for.

I grabbed my dagger and turned to face the two of them. Before I could steady myself, a third fighter joined the fray. He was smaller but no less dangerous. His movements were quick and darting, his strikes precise. I blocked one, then another, but I couldn't keep up. Not with two more advancing from opposite sides. They were overwhelming me, forcing me back, their blows raining down like a storm.

I stumbled, the dirt loose beneath my boots, and knew with a sick certainty that I couldn't hold out much longer. My arms burned. My vision blurred. The cheers of the crowd were a mocking roar in my ears.

To add insult to injury, a fourth figure entered the arena. Actually, this fighter entered from the stands, not the gates. Which was odd.

Still, the odds were not in my favor. Four against one. There was no way I could win. No way I could survive.

Until I saw the fury in those dark eyes.

Dark eyes that I had first seen on my ninth birthday in the stables. That hair I'd run my fingers through. Those lips that I had kissed over and over and—

Blood splattered on those lips as a long sword tore

through first the lean man, then doubled over to slice through the woman, and then point at the large man.

The fourth warrior moved like a force of nature. His blade caught the spotlight as he struck down the third attacker. The crowd erupted, their cheers deafening. I barely heard them. All I could see was him.

"Jorge?"

CHAPTER ELEVEN

JORGE

She was taller now. Her frame leaner but still strong. Her wild curls were bound back, though a few strands had escaped to frame her face. Her violet hair caught the spotlight, shimmering like a living flame. It was her eyes that captured me.

Those sharp, determined blue eyes that hadn't softened with time. If anything, they burned brighter, fiercer. I forgot to breathe as we stared at each other.

Blood dripped from my blade. Screams rose from the ground where the other fighters who'd dared raise arms against her were crying over their lost limbs and the life slowly seeping from their bodies. I heard nothing but the soft utterance of my name from her perfect lips.

"Jorge?"

How had I thought she'd forgotten me? My name on her breath was a spark. That spark rekindled the promise between us. It caught quickly, scorching the distance between us until that vacuum of air was no more.

She reached for me, and I noticed her hands were smudged with dirt. The skin of her index finger had a cut. I knew it had come from one of the thugs. I wanted to turn and take another limb as penance for daring to mar the masterpiece that was her body.

Their murders would have to wait. Because I couldn't take my eyes off her. Couldn't turn from the center of my orbit.

"Jorge?"

Yes, it was me. Of course it was me. I'd promised I'd go wherever she was. I'd spent the last three years gutting trolls and fighting my way up the food chain so that I could be where I knew she would turn up. I never suspected for a moment that she would be on the very grounds I'd nearly died on.

"Jorge!"

I didn't see the attack until it was too late.

A blade whispered through the air. I turned just in

time to block the tip with my forearm—its deadly edge howling past, a breath away from my throat. Pain shot through my body as the impact jarred my prosthetic. I held firm. Then countered with a strike of my own.

My attacker staggered back. Blood dripped from a gash across his chest. Unfortunately, I wasn't fast enough to avoid the next opponent.

A blade came toward me again, and I braced for the hit—only it didn't come. Instead, there was a metallic clang. I turned to see Charlotte standing beside me, the beautiful blade I'd made for her raised, her expression fierce.

Her movements were fluid. Each strike precise. Every lethal movement graceful. She wasn't just holding her own in the fight—she was dominating.

The last of our enemies fell. Their weapons clattered to the ground as they crumpled at Charlotte's feet. The arena erupted into cheers. It was all a distant hum in my ears. All I could see was her.

Charlotte turned to me, her chest heaving with exertion, her face flushed. We picked up where we'd left off in our reunion; we just stared at each other. The weight of years and distance and pain hung between us.

She moved, closing the space between us in a heartbeat. "Let me see."

I was a child again. Holding up my scrapes and wounds to her. Hearing her scolding tone as she gave me the care I'd been so sorely deprived of my entire miserable life. Hungry for the numbness her magic would flood inside me. Every time Charlotte took away my pain, she left something of herself inside me. It became my addiction. I'd been so long without my fix.

For three years, I had been holding her hand. In the trenches of war, in the bitter cold of the barracks, through every brutal skirmish, I had felt her fingers wrapped around mine. She had been my anchor, my strength, the reason I kept moving forward when everything else tried to break me.

The moment Charlotte's fingers brushed against mine, my world realigned. My brain connected the memory to my body, filling in the pieces that had frayed over time. I had forgotten the way her warmth seeped into my palm. How her thumb always moved in slow circles over my knuckles. How the knuckles of our other four fingers aligned so perfectly. I had forgotten how I could feel the subtle rhythm of her pulse in my palm because her hand was slightly smaller than mine. The top part of her wrist came to rest in the bottom part of my palm.

Then she jerked from my hold. My phantom limb clenched at the loss, grasping at nothing, desperate to hold on to what had always been there. A sharp, gutting ache spread through my chest, worse than any blade had ever carved into me. The connection that had carried me through every battle, every wound, every moment of agony—severed.

Charlotte stared at my empty hand.

No—not my hand. The thing that had replaced it.

Undisguised horror flickered across her face as she took in the smooth, dark metal where flesh should have been. The fingers I had reforged, the ones I had spent years perfecting so they could move, flex, and function like they were my own—she looked at them as if they were something unnatural. As if they were something unworthy of her touch.

Then, as if catching herself, she blinked and looked away, as though she could pretend this moment hadn't just cracked something irreparable between us. She reached for me, pulling me into her arms. I went to her. Of course I did. I was the moth. She could burn me alive, and I would thank her for it.

Her lips met mine, demanding as always. Her hands wrapped around my neck and pulled me closer as though I was her due—which I was. Her body was flush against mine. All that was left to do was take what was being offered to me. My hands obeyed, and a new memory was formed. One where Charlotte's fingers in mine were replaced with the firm roundness of her ass in my palms.

Together, we deepened the kiss. I poured every unspoken word, every unshed tear, every unfulfilled longing into that single, perfect moment. She was here, she was alive, and I felt whole.

"Attention, competitors and spectators," the announcer's voice boomed over the loudspeakers, cold and devoid of emotion. "We have a situation. One of the combatants has entered the arena illegally. Both the illegal participant and his partner will be disqualified and removed from the Games immediately."

The cheers died down as a wave of confusion rippled through the stands. A chorus of boos rang out. The crowd's displeasure didn't change the official's ruling.

Guards marched forward. Their hands reached for Charlotte to take her away from me. Charlotte palmed her blade.

I turned toward the announcer's platform, scanning the high crystalline screen where the voice originated. I raised my arm, prosthetics gleaming under the twin suns.

"I am a survivor of the Convergence Games. My name is in the records. By your own rules, all former competitors are eligible to return."

The arena fell into silence, the murmurs dying as all eyes turned to the announcer's box. The weight of a thousand stares pressed down on us. Beside me, Charlotte reached for my prosthetic hand. The knowledge that we both might lose our lives in moments felt less important than her acceptance of what I had become. The warmth of her skin seared through the cold metal, sending a jolt through the mechanical nerves, tricking my mind into believing I was whole again.

"We will... review the records. For now, both contestants will proceed to the barracks. Further decisions will be announced."

CHAPTER TWELVE

CHARLOTTE

Jorge's hand wrapped around mine, pulling me through the chaos behind the scenes of the Convergence Games. I didn't mind the manhandling in the slightest. Not when I was doing my own version of it to him.

I couldn't stop touching him. My fingers curled tighter around his, the occasional brush of my arm against his. He felt so different.

Harder. Stronger. But not just in the way his body had filled out with his lean muscle, honed into something lethal.

Jorge had always been pliable when we were young. Soft where I was sharp. Yielding where I was unmovable. He had been the boy who bent beneath the weight of expectation, who never resisted when pushed, who absorbed every blow life threw at him and kept going.

But now…

Now when I touched him, I felt no give beneath my fingers. His body was no longer something that could be shaped by the world around him. It had been sculpted by battle, by survival, by his own will.

No, Jorge wouldn't bend anymore. And gods help me, that thrilled me.

Heat coiled in my stomach. This was the same boy who used to kneel at my feet, who once followed me with wide, reverent eyes, who never resisted when I pulled him into a dark place and made him kiss every part of my body. Now there was steel in him, literally.

I had never liked the enhancements that warriors brought into the Games. Prosthetics made of gleaming steel and arcane tech, turning flesh into something unnatural. It had always unsettled me, likely because I was a fairy, and we had our prejudices against metals.

And yet Jorge's fingers wrapped around mine with such familiar precision that if I closed my eyes, I wouldn't have known the difference.

It felt like him.

Because it was him.

I ran my thumb over his knuckles, expecting cold metal, expecting that jarring difference between man and machine. There was warmth pulsing beneath the surface like a heartbeat. His fingers tightened ever so slightly, responding to my touch the way they always had.

The lean muscle in his arms was nothing like the bulky builds of the warriors surrounding us. Jorge's muscles were deliberate, honed with precision, as though his body had been carved from steel and tempered in fire.

They'd found his name in the records and officially welcomed him as a return competitor. The Games were over for the night, and we were sent with the other survivors to the warriors' quarters. Jorge's gait as we walked through what could only be described as a small village was confident, his stride long and purposeful, as though each step declared his place in this space. His clothes were finer than anything he'd ever worn back home, tailored to fit his frame.

I couldn't stop staring at the stubble on his jaw. He'd never had stubble before. It suited him—too well.

If I hadn't known the feel of him down to my very bones, I might have thought this was someone else entirely.

The way people looked at him only added to the dissonance. Guards moved out of our path with a snap of respect, their heads bowing in deference. A murmur followed us, rippling through the crowd. I caught the word "Commander" more than once.

He swept us into one of the cabins, closing the heavy door behind us. A large bed draped in rich fabrics dominated one corner. A sitting area was tucked by an unlit fireplace. I spied the glint of a marble-tiled bathing room beyond.

Before I could marvel—or demand answers—Jorge turned, his expression dark and thunderous.

"What were you thinking?"

I stumbled back a step, my mouth opening and closing like a fish as I tried to process his anger. Jorge had never raised his voice at me before. Never.

His hand was at my throat, the prosthetic one. His chest pressed against mine. His eyes were fire.

My brain fizzled. He was yelling at me, and all I wanted to do was kiss him. No, I wanted to push him down on the bed, sit on his face, and have him yell into my core. Oh, I was wet thinking about it.

But I knew I couldn't move his hand. He had me pinned. At his mercy. I pressed my thighs together and got no relief.

"I came to find you."

His jaw worked. He looked at my mouth, my lips. His nostrils flared.

I leaned forward, trying to capture his lips. He held

me in place. I didn't like that. I didn't like not being able to have him.

"You shouldn't be here," he said.

That made no sense. He was here. I was supposed to be wherever he was.

"You were supposed to be at the summer castle," he continued.

"How do you know that?"

"Because I suggested it to him."

I stopped struggling. Jorge let me go. He paced away from me. It gave me a look at his tight ass. And his stride. His thighs had never been that thick, that strong. His shoulder blades were bigger. It was like he had been rebuilt to my every fantasy. I hadn't known I wanted him this way until he was standing in front of me with so much power coming from him.

"Wait. You suggested what to who?"

"Do you even understand what you've done?" His voice cracked like a whip, his dark eyes burning as he stopped just short of me. His chest rose and fell with the force of his breaths. He was so close, so overwhelming. "You threw yourself into the Convergence Games like you were invincible. Like your life was expendable. You could have died! Do you know what it's like to look up at the crystal viewer and see you in the lineup, knowing exactly what those games are designed to do? Knowing what they could do to you?"

There was a lot to unpack there, but there was only one thing that I truly wanted to know. "Where were you?"

"Where was I? I was where you were supposed to be today."

"I was supposed to be meeting the Beast Prince."

"Correct."

He'd said he knew I was going to be at the summer castle, that he had suggested it to *him*. "You were with the Beast Prince?"

Jorge threw aside his cape to reveal the insignia of the Solmane army. I wasn't one to understand medals, but he had a lot of them. Once again, I heard the term *commander* in my head.

"You're in the army?"

"After I survived the games, they gave me a choice. Return to the competition or become a conscript. If I played again and won in the next games, I could have my freedom. Winning was a gamble. Joining the army put me closer to where I knew you would be."

"You could've died."

"Then I would've figured out how to haunt you. There's nothing I wouldn't do to get close to you."

"You fought trolls?"

"I did. I made my way up the ranks and got closer and closer to the prince."

"Commander?"

"Second in command. Prince Adom's most trusted warrior. I was at his side today when he came to… meet you. Instead, I found an imposter in your place."

"Belle. Poor thing."

"I think he's quite taken with her."

I reached for Jorge's hand, the prosthetic one. "Is that where you got this?"

"I made it myself. No iron."

"I wouldn't care if it was iron. I'd burn for you."

"Fuck, Charlotte," he sighed, closing his prosthetic fingers around mine.

"Yes. I want you to do exactly that. I want you to fuck me."

The feel of his real fingers wrapped tightly around mine was the last memory I had of him. I didn't let go, even after they severed his hand. They had to pry it away from me.

There was no one to disentangle him from me now. I flung myself at him. He was caught off guard, but he caught me.

I captured his lips, and he let me.

I drank him down, and he let me.

I bit his lip, and he let me.

He was Jorge. He was mine. And I had him back.

CHAPTER THIRTEEN

JORGE

Her lips were fire. No, not fire—something hotter, something that consumed and left no trace of the life I'd born for the time that we were apart. Charlotte kissed me with a hunger that matched the ache I'd carried for three years. Her hands tangled in my hair. Her body pressed so close to mine I could feel her heart pounding against my chest.

It felt like a dream—no, a waking nightmare that had finally shattered. The years of fighting, the endless bloodshed, the sleepless nights staring into the dark and wondering if she was sad—they all faded into nothing. All that mattered now was the reality of her in my arms, the taste of her kiss, the weight of her command, as if she owned me.

Because she did.

I'd been born for this—for her. To love her, to protect her, to keep her safe.

The thought of what she'd been through, the danger she'd willingly walked into, turned my blood to molten steel. My hands tightened around her waist as the realization broke through the haze of desire.

I broke the kiss, pressing my forehead to hers as I tried to steady my breathing. "Did you volunteer for the Games?"

"I ran away when we got to the summer castle. It was the first time in three years they left me unguarded, so I ran to find you."

She aimed for my mouth again, but I needed to know more. "You ran to the Games?"

"I ran into warriors on the road. Kael Drakos, can you believe it? He's awful."

That was a fantasy I hadn't wanted to dispel for her. Drakos was a womanizing, cheating brute, like I'd always suspected. I'd had it confirmed in my short time in the Games with women running from his quarters, tears streaming down their faces and their clothes torn.

"He tried to take advantage of me."

"He what?"

"So I broke his arm. Then his henchmen knocked me out. When I woke up, I was here."

Rage flared in my chest. I was going to kill him. First, I forced myself to take a deep breath, to focus on the fact that Charlotte was here, alive, and unbroken.

For now.

But she was in the Games. That made her anything but safe.

"We need to get you cleaned up."

"I'd rather get dirty with you."

My cock had been asleep for three years. It sprang painfully to life with that. My ever-present need to care for her won the day. "Let me see to you first."

It was formed as a question, but I wasn't taking suggestions. I lifted her off the ground, scooping her into my arms.

Charlotte gasped. Her gaze went wide as she glanced at the floor, then at me. I'd never been strong enough to do this before. She was about to see that I was no longer that weak boy. I was all man, with some enhancements I'd personally engineered just for her.

I carried her to the bathing room that was the second room in these lodgings. That was one thing about the Games: if you survived, you were treated well. Lodgings and two meals a day both during the

Games and the three years between tournaments. But that was only if you survived.

Charlotte and I had won today. But the game we played wasn't over. The Sun and Moon Gauntlet was a two-day event. There was still more fighting to do. I'd worry about tomorrow when it came.

The pipes groaned as I turned on one of the faucets. A steady stream of lukewarm water cascaded down into the basin below. Charlotte held still for me as I unfastened the stays on her dress. Her gaze never left mine, as though she was afraid I'd disappear from her sight if she looked away.

I felt the exact same. I warred between wanting to gaze at her, wanting to touch her, and wanting to hear her voice. I realized I could do all three.

"You're all right?" I asked as I tugged her arms free of the dirty garment, my fingers brushing the warm skin I uncovered.

"I missed you so much. I was aching for three years without you."

She spoke the words that were in my heart. She was everything—my light in the darkness, my reason for fighting, my reason for breathing. I would do whatever it took to keep her safe, even if it meant facing every nightmare this damned tournament could throw at us.

Her wings fluttered out as the dress slipped from her shoulders. I was more interested in them than her bared breasts. There was truth to men being hypnotized by a fairy's wings. In the capital, many fairies walked around with their wings out like it was nothing. That didn't mean they didn't get pestered in the streets.

I'd never once been tempted. Not when I had seen and touched and tasted the most perfect pair of wings on the planet.

Charlotte shivered as I soaped them. The silken membranes gleamed under the warm water. The faint iridescence caught the light with every careful stroke of my fingers. I worked the lather in gently, massaging along the fine structure, mindful of the tender joints where wing met back.

I knew where her sensitive spots were. The slightest brush along the lower ridge sent a ripple through her body. My hands slowed, tracing over the intricate veins that shimmered just beneath the surface, following their natural patterns as though they were etched into my memory.

Her wings quivered as I rinsed the suds away, the weight of water making them heavier, drooping slightly under the cascade. I caught them, lifting one carefully, letting the droplets roll off my fingertips. They were so much stronger than they looked but still impossibly delicate. Like her. Like everything about her that made her both fierce and breathtaking.

Her breasts had grown. They were fuller in my

hands. Her ass too. It had gotten stronger. We both were warriors now, each determined to protect the other.

As I washed away the dirt and blood from her perfect skin, she stood still. Oh, she squirmed, but she did not move away. She had never moved away from my touch.

"Please, Jorge."

"Shhh, my starlight."

Now was not the time for what she wanted. We had to plan. We had to strategize. Maybe I could get us out with my position in the military. But then Prince Adom would know he had the wrong bride, and they would take her from me.

No, the Games were likely the best place for us to hide while the Prince of Solmane took his vows with the imposter.

"Please."

Charlotte's gaze was on my prosthetic hand. The look was heated. It was the same look as when she'd come to me in the middle of the night, when we were barely full grown. The look that only I could ease.

This woman was my world. I would bend space and time for her. All she was asking was for me to offer her release. It was what I was made for. It was her right to ask me for pleasure. And so I gave it to her.

I pressed my finger to her core.

"Yes, Jorge."

The prosthetic was connected to my brain. I only had to give it a command. The metal came to life like it was sentient and it wanted to do this.

Charlotte gasped as I sent the warmth of a single digit straight to her clit. She moaned as my attachment began to hum. I'd made it with her in mind. Though I'd never actually used this feature. So I'd never had the occasion to calibrate it.

She orgasmed in five seconds flat. Her body jerked and spasmed as though it had been struck by lightning. She stopped breathing for five seconds after that as she tried to regain control of her limbs.

But my girl was a greedy fae. One orgasm had never been enough for her. I kicked her thighs apart. Her legs were weak from her first release, but now I was strong enough to support her.

I hefted her up against the shower wall until her core was flush against my face. I draped her thighs over my shoulders. Her heels hit my back. Her knees pressed against my ears.

I took a deep inhale of my favorite scent, realizing that there were fresh new notes that hadn't been there before. I released a heated exhale against her open folds that had her shivering. Then I dug into my meal. I gorged myself on the nectar I'd been deprived of, the nectar I'd fought for for the last three years.

Charlotte's nails dug into my shoulders. She began shaking. Her heels dug into my back. Her knees pressed against my temples. I pulled a deeper orgasm from her, one that had her whole body shaking. And I didn't stop. I was never going to stop now that I had her back.

This was how we would exist in this world. Charlotte would be wrapped around my face as I walked, as we ate, as we slept. Because I was in paradise.

I leaned her against the shower walls and tilted her hips forward. I pressed harder to capture the sweet honey that gushed from between her thighs. I licked up every last drop and coaxed more to come down from the treasure trove inside her core. We stayed that way in the shower until her skin was a shriveled prune, her voice hoarse from an hour of moaning, and my tongue was sated with the taste of her.

CHAPTER FOURTEEN

CHARLOTTE

It was exactly like I remembered; Jorge suckled my clit, licked into my channel, and nibbled at my folds until I'd passed out. Which pissed me off because I had been dreaming of his cock for three long years.

I woke to a wet dream of him inside me. Jorge was long, that I knew from when I sat on his face and leaned back as he made my hips convulse all over his nose and chin. I'd reach behind myself for purchase and a time or two I'd met with the hard length of him. His weapon rested low on his thigh and gave me something fierce to hold on to.

But Jorge rarely let me bring him to completion. When I managed to get my hands on him, he'd flip me over and dive back into my core until I was a whimpering mess. Or I passed out. Which is what happened during my shower.

I woke up clean and refreshed. My core was swollen like a sated hog. It was somewhat uncomfortable to close my thighs with my nether region so fat. As full as I felt, it wasn't enough. I wanted Jorge inside of me.

Not his fingers. Not his tongue. I wanted his cock.

Jorge lay behind me, his body curled around mine, his hands tucked around my hips, holding me securely to him.

The first rays of the two suns spilled through the cracks in the curtains. His warmth surrounded me, his chest rising and falling in a steady rhythm that lulled my racing thoughts. Everything felt right—perfect.

Bruises lined my body. My muscles ached in ways I hadn't thought possible. All of that faded to a dull whisper compared to the feel of him. His strength was an unfamiliar weight against me. His arm, once fragile and broken, now held me like it could carry the world. I ran my fingers over the hard muscle of his biceps. His forearm ended in pliable metal.

His hand had been taken from him. He had been

taken from me. But we were back together and somehow put together. Even with the bruising and the swelling, I felt perfectly healed.

I tilted my head up to look back at him. His eyes were closed, his face relaxed. Goddess, how I had missed his face. There were so many details that I'd forgotten about him.

The way his lashes were absurdly long, casting delicate shadows on his cheeks. The faint scar along his left temple, a pale line against his tanned skin, a reminder of one of the many times he'd thrown himself into danger for my sake. The way his lips, always slightly chapped from being out in the sun, curved in the faintest of smiles even when he was at rest.

I had missed him. Missed this. The boy in the stables was now a man. And I'd missed it. I wanted to find the Beast Prince and gut the monster for taking this all from me.

Jorge's eyes opened, those familiar dark pools meeting mine. I smiled up at him. He smiled back. Then I attacked.

I lunged for him, aiming to catch him off guard. My hands darted for his shoulders, my knees pressed to the mattress as I tried to wrestle my way on top of him.

Jorge moved faster than I expected. With barely any effort, he caught my wrists and twisted, flipping me onto my back, leaving me breathless. He loomed over me, pinning my arms above my head with ease. His grip was firm, unyielding. I felt the raw strength he now carried.

And I liked it.

"What are you doing, starlight?" he asked.

"I was trying to have my way with you."

A slow smile spread across his handsome face. With his free hand, the one with the prosthetic, he reached for a lock of my hair. I arched my chin into his hand like a feline. The feel of his mech hand was soft, cooler than the rest of him. But if I closed my eyes, I'd know it was him. Also because he smelled faintly of me.

This wasn't the Jorge I remembered. This wasn't the boy who used to falter when I teased him, who used to blush when I smiled too brightly. This was a man, battle-hardened and confident. The realization sent a wave of heat rolling through me.

"Since when are you so strong?"

"Since the world stopped letting me be weak. So don't test me, Charlotte."

"I don't want to test you. I want to fuck you."

He rubbed his thumb across my bottom lip. "This mouth—"

"Wants your cock." I snared his thumb with my tongue.

With a deliberate slowness, I released his thumb. His grip on my hands slackened. I reached for his face. I placed kisses where my fingers traced. Jorge let me kiss him. He was so focused on my lips meeting his flesh that he lost track of my hand, making its way beneath the sheets.

He still wore trousers. I snared his zipper with the tips of my fingers. Jorge's body tensed, a statue carved from surprise and then anticipation. My hands deftly slid beneath the fabric. The heat of him seared my palm as I wrapped my fingers around his cock, already hard and pulsing with need.

A soft groan escaped his lips as I began to stroke him. Each movement of my hand was hungry, learning the shape and feel of him all over again. His hips bucked.

"Charlotte..." His voice was a rough whisper, telling me to behave.

I had no such plans. I deepened the kiss until he was pliant on top of me. Then, in a move I'd learned watching the Convergence Games, I flipped our positions. He crashed into the mattress on his back, and I mounted him. This time, I ducked his attempts to snare me by getting low on his body.

I was at his hips when he grabbed for me. All he got in his mechanical hand was my hair. I also got what I grabbed for: his cock.

With one last, firm stroke of my hand, I leaned forward. The taste of him was intoxicating, a blend of salt and skin that had my heart hammering against my ribs. My mouth enveloped him, warm and wet, and I took him in deeper.

I felt it the moment he gave up. His fingers threaded through my hair, holding on but not guiding. A silent admission of surrender. Each bob of my head, each swirl of my tongue, unraveled him further until the lines of control blurred into nothingness. I worshipped him with fervor, determined to claim every gasp and shudder as my own.

He tried to pull me away before he reached his climax. I held firm. I took him as deep as I could go and suckled.

Jorge let out a strangled cry as he spilled into my mouth.

I kept suckling. Swallowing him down. Licking up the excess that managed to dribble down his length. I dabbed at my chin and caught those dregs, too. I let none of him escape me.

It was better than when he had his mouth on me. The power of it. The command of it. I wanted to do it again.

I reached for his semi-hard cock. Preparing to take him again. He never let me rest at one orgasm. Turn-about was fair play.

Somehow, he found the strength to hold me at bay. He pressed his length directly against my core but not into it.

"Can you feel this?"

"Yes," I cheered, finally about to get what I wanted.

"It's yours. I'm yours."

"Yes, you are. You are mine. And I am yours."

"You are my constant, Charlotte. You are my starlight, my guide out of the darkness."

"You will never be in darkness again because I will never leave your side."

He kissed me then. Tenderly, deeply. Even though I closed my eyes to savor the feel of his lips against mine, all I saw was the light of him above me. I reached for that lightning rod between his legs.

Jorge pulled away from me again. "You can have this once we win the Games."

I groaned, flopping back against the mattress. "The Games can wait. I want the prize I truly fought for."

"I'll let you have your way with me after we've won."

"Why do we have to win? Can't we just leave?"

Jorge rose on his forearm to look down at me. "Charlotte, there's no leaving the Games. There are only three options; you win, you die, or you are conscripted."

I'd watched these games for as long as I could remember, and I don't think I ever knew that. I only knew what became of the winners. I paid little attention to the losers who died. Even less attention to those who survived but weren't on the winner's platform in the end.

"Can't we try to escape?"

"If we escaped, which has never been done before, then we'll face Adom."

"He's Adom to you, then?"

"If we weren't hardened warriors, he might call me his best friend. Although yesterday, I had every intention of stealing his bride from him. So I doubt he'll ask me to stand up for him during the wedding ceremony."

"It wouldn't have been stealing. I would've never married him. The moment they lead me out of Evergrove, I never intended to go back. I never intended to meet him. I only intended to find you."

Jorge's throat worked. Had he doubted me? Foolish man; he was mine. I was not leaving this world without him. At least not without having him. And there was the real possibility that one or both of us might not survive today.

"The least you can do is let me touch it again."

"No." He smirked.

"Just put the tip in. You're already so close."

I moved toward him. Jorge got off the bed. He was gloriously naked, and his cock was no longer semi-hard. It was definitively hard.

"Cock tease."

"I need you fighting mad when we go in there, not sated."

His words sobered me. He was right, of course. He always was when it came to keeping me safe. As much as I wanted to lose myself in the quiet moments with him, there was a battle waiting for us—a fight we couldn't afford to lose.

CHAPTER FIFTEEN

JORGE

The morning sun was harsh against my skin, baking the dust and sweat into a second layer over me as I walked. My legs felt sluggish, each step harder than the last, as though they'd turned to lead after the morning spent resisting Charlotte's advances.

My cock was the lightning rod she'd called it. I was surprised the eager thing wasn't burning a hole in my pants to get to her. My brain wasn't fully operational yet. It kept trying to spark to life. After that cataclysmic orgasm I'd had from her mouth on me, I didn't have enough juice to start my engines fully.

The fairy princess had drained me dry. And yet she pouted beside me, constantly stealing glances at the very erect rod making itself known in my pants. My cock wanted her. My tongue wanted her. I wanted her.

But wanting her wasn't the same as taking her. Not here. Not now.

The last time we'd gotten comfortable, the world had reminded me how easily it could rip everything away. I had lost my hand, which I would trade again and again if it meant saving her. But the price of three years apart? That had been too much. Too cruel.

The memory of those years—the games, the pain, the nights I thought I'd never see her again—sharpened my focus. These games weren't a stage for idle fantasies; they were a graveyard waiting to claim its next resident.

And beyond the arena, there was Adom. I couldn't ignore the shadow of the prince, the man who trusted me, who might yet discover the ultimate betrayal. If he'd realized the fairy princess at his side was a fraud, what then? Was the palace even looking for the real Charlotte now?

Beside me, Charlotte's hand was warm in mine, her fingers lacing through mine like a lifeline. The quiet strength in her grip steadied me, even as my mind churned with unease. Her defiance, her fire—it was what I loved about her. But it was also what made me fear for her in this place.

The village of competitors stretched before us as we walked toward the arena. It was just as I remembered: a patchwork of desperation and chaos. The sounds of crying filtered through the air. Laughter, too, sharp and wild, the kind that came from the lips of people who had accepted their own doom. And then there were the sounds of pleasure, of people fucking like it was their last day alive, because for some it was.

Charlotte looked around, her chin lifted, her expression steely. I knew that look. She wasn't afraid, not like the others. She was determined. But determination didn't make you invincible. I kept my senses sharp, my eyes scanning the crowd for anyone who might see her as more than a competitor. For anyone who might see her as a threat.

Two soldiers emerged from the shadows of the village entrance, their armor catching the sunlight in sharp flashes. They moved with purpose, their gazes sweeping over the area until they landed on us. Recognition dawned—but for which one of us?

My body tensed, instinct firing through me like a second heartbeat. My hand twitched at my side, the mechanical fingers humming faintly, ready. I pulled

Charlotte closer, keeping her half-hidden behind me, and met the soldiers' eyes with a steady glare.

"Commander, it really is you," said the taller one, giving me a salute.

The thicker one followed suit, his fist going to his heart and thumping his chest three times. "Who knew one of the most decorated fighters in all of Solmane came from the Games as a conscript? May we escort you to the arena?"

Neither one of them had even spared a glance at Charlotte. They likely thought she was some doxy I'd used for the night. I didn't disabuse them of that notion.

The announcer's voice boomed over the din of the crowd. "Entering now, a warrior of Solmane and veteran of the Troll Wars—Jorge Terran! Soldier of the Iron Sun Brigade, Commander to the Lion Prince!"

The crowd erupted into deafening applause, their cheers rolling like thunder over the coliseum. My face appeared on the large crystal viewer that would broadcast all over the developed parts of Lunaterra.

I fought the urge to pull Charlotte back into the shadows with me. There was no way Adom wouldn't know I was here. Maybe trying to run had been the better choice. Too late for that now.

The gates groaned open. The arena's blinding light spilled over us. The roar of the crowd surged again. Heat and sound crashed over me in waves. The smell of sweat, blood, and the tang of scorched earth filled my nostrils as we were thrust into the battlefield for the next game.

Charlotte gripped the dagger I'd made her all those years ago. There was no fear in her, only focus. Goddess, she was brave—reckless, too, but brave. I stayed close, my body coiled like a spring, my prosthetic hand rolling through its catalog of weapons that would keep her safe.

The first wave came fast—too fast for some. A massive figure charged toward us, their armor dented and blood-streaked from previous rounds. I stepped in front of Charlotte, my blade slicing the air in a smooth arc. The fighter's weapon clanged against mine. The vibration jarred up my arm, but I didn't falter. I pressed forward, forcing them back. Nothing was getting past me. Not to her.

But I wasn't perfect. One competitor did slip by me —a wiry opponent with wickedly fast reflexes. I spun to intercept them. My steps faltered as my gaze locked on Charlotte.

For the past three years that I'd pictured her in my mind, it was always the pliant Charlotte after I'd spent at least an hour between her thighs. I'd forgotten that she had trained herself. That she'd watched these games and practiced the moves like they were her religion.

All that devotion paid off. She was magnificent.

Every movement was a dance, every strike pure poetry. Her lavender skin glowed in the sunlight. Her hair whipped around her like a silken halo. If her wings hadn't been bound to her back, she would have stunned them all into offering their necks just to get close to her.

Charlotte was strong and quick. She darted past her opponent's defenses with the grace I'd seen her exude at stately dinner parties. Her blade sang as it sliced through the air.

I forgot everything as I stood still and watched her. I forgot my mission, my fears, my doubts. There was only her. Beautiful, deadly, breathtaking Charlotte.

More fighters came. I held them back. They needed to wait their turn to dance with my beauty and her blade.

I didn't deliver killing blows to the waiting suitors, only deflected and delayed. One by one, they tried to pass. One by one, I let them.

Charlotte didn't need my protection—she was handling them all, her blade a blur, her confidence a beacon in the chaos. I bit my bottom lip as I watched. My cock got harder with every slice. I got more and more turned on the bloodier her blade got.

CHAPTER SIXTEEN

CHARLOTTE

Three competitors surged toward me. The first came at me with a double-edged blade. I sidestepped, twisting just enough to let his momentum carry him past me. My dagger flashed, and he hit the ground before he even registered the cut.

The second fighter was already on me. Her axe arced toward my head, the blade whistling through the air. I dropped low, rolling beneath the strike and coming up behind her. Before she could turn, I lashed out, my dagger slicing through the straps of her armor.

She stumbled, unbalanced, and I struck again, this time sending her sprawling.

I turned to face the third. He wasn't coming for me. He was locked in a battle with Jorge. But Jorge was toying with him, his gaze on me.

"Are you ready for this one?"

Jorge gave the fighter a shove toward me. When the fighter regained their footing, they came at me. As we fought, all I could hear was Jorge's voice.

"Isn't she magnificent? It's like she's dancing with him. You should see her on the dance floor. I'm almost sad for you that you won't get that joy."

Jorge had the remaining fighter at sword point. His blade hovered just above the man's throat. Yet he wasn't delivering a killing blow.

When the third fighter came at me, I drove my dagger into their shoulder. They fell to their knees, clutching the wound. They didn't get up again.

I turned my attention back to Jorge. He gave me a beatific grin. His arm was outstretched, a blade extending from the middle finger of his prosthetic, aimed at a fourth competitor's neck.

The field was smaller now. The weaker competitors had been eliminated. Some by choice, others by force. Across the expanse, a group of fighters stood in a tight huddle, their eyes fixed on me. Recognition struck me.

It was them. The ones who had thrown me into this nightmare. Drakos's crew.

Kael Drakos stood across from me, his silhouette a warped reflection of the man I'd once admired. The towering champion of the Sun and Moon Gauntlet, the fighter who had claimed victory time and time again, now bore a cruel smirk that tugged at his scarred lips. The left arm that had been broken by my own blade now gleamed with mech enhancements. He rolled his shoulders. The sound of grinding gears set my teeth on edge.

Beside me, Jorge stepped into my peripheral vision. He quickly dispensed of the fourth competitor with a blow to the back of the man's head. As the fallen warrior crumpled, Jorge stepped up beside me.

He didn't draw his blade. He didn't launch himself in front of me. Instead, he looked at me, his dark eyes soft despite the tension etched across his face.

"Do you want my help?"

Another man wouldn't have bothered to ask. Another man would've rushed forward, blade swinging, eager to claim the glory or shield me from harm. But not Jorge.

He wasn't any man. He was a hero. Heroes always put their heroine's needs first.

"No," I said softly, shaking my head. "He's mine."

Jorge nodded, stepping back. He sheathed his prosthetic, returning it to the digit that had stroked me to ecstasy last night. He crossed one leg over the other as he rested against a beam.

Trust. That's what it was between us. Not just love, but an unshakable trust that made me feel invincible.

I turned my gaze back to Kael.

The hardened warrior watched us with an amused expression. "I'm not going to kill you. I'm going to take the spoils you denied me the other night."

I ignored the has-been, planting my feet and leveling my blade. I wasn't going to win this for myself. I was going to win it for Jorge—for the man who had stood by me, fought for me, and believed in me when I hadn't known who I was. Now I knew exactly who I was: I was Jorge's.

Kael moved first. He wasn't moving like a drunkard today. He lunged with the speed of a predator. His mech-enhanced arm shot out, aiming for my side. I twisted, narrowly avoiding the strike. The weight of his attack left a divot in the ground where I'd stood.

I darted around him, light on my feet. My blade slashed toward his exposed flank. He blocked it with his enhanced arm. The clash of metal against metal reverberated up my arm. The force of it jarred me, but I held steady.

Kael was strong, but he was slower than he'd been

before. His mech might have been powerful, but it was poorly maintained, the joints stiff and the movements predictable. I could use that against him.

"You've lost your edge, old man," I taunted, darting back to avoid another swing. "All that metal, and you've grown clumsy with age."

He growled, his good hand tightening around his weapon. "We'll see how clumsy I am when I'm standing over your broken, naked body."

He lunged again. This time, I met him head-on. Our blades clashed, sparks flying as metal screamed against metal. My muscles burned, every swing and parry pushing me closer to my limit.

I refused to back down. I ducked under his arm, aiming a slash at his leg. The blade caught, biting into flesh and sending him stumbling.

"Stay down, Drakos," I said, my voice steady despite my racing heart. "This fight is over."

He didn't listen. With a roar, he surged forward, his mechanical arm swinging wildly. I sidestepped, bringing my blade down hard on the joint of his mech. The metal cracked, sparks flying as the limb seized and hung useless at his side.

There were gasps in the crowd. Then silence. Then a roar of cheers as bloodlust took over the onlookers. They were cheering. For me.

But Kael Drakos had never been a man to accept defeat.

I felt it before I saw it—the shift in the air, the sudden tension in the crowd. A flicker of movement in my periphery.

Then the glint of a blade.

Too fast. Too close.

I barely had time to turn before the wicked curve of his dagger sliced through the air, aimed straight for my throat. A cheap shot, a killing blow meant to take me out, even in his failure.

There was no time to move.

A metallic whirr split the air, followed by a sickening crack.

Drakos froze, his body jerking. His eyes widened in shock as he looked down at his own blade now embedded in his chest. But how?

There was a hum of energy coming from behind me. Like a ray of sunlight shining on a part of your body. Or how it felt when going through a portal and energy surrounded you.

Jorge had his hand up in a stop motion. A yellow glow pulsed from his hand. I don't know how, but I knew whatever had happened, it had come from Jorge.

Drakos made a choked, wheezing sound, as though trying to form words. Then his body sagged, and he crumpled at my feet.

The crowd erupted into a frenzy. I barely heard them. My hand was being raised in the air as the new victor of the Sun and Moon Games. I didn't care about the victory, just the prize. And he was right beside me.

CHAPTER SEVENTEEN

JORGE

The crowd erupted, their voices a thunderous roar. Blood pounded in my ears as it ran from Kael Drakos' empty chest. I turned to see Charlotte, unsure of what I was expecting to see. I'd just killed her hero.

Her dagger gleamed in the sunlight. The metal was dim in comparison to the brilliance of the smile she arrowed directly to my heart. She stepped over the disgraced warrior to get to me.

The cameras were trained on us, the crystal screens

broadcasting every moment. I didn't care. Let them watch. I pulled her close and kissed her.

We'd done it. We'd won. We were finally free: free to be ourselves, together.

Her lips were soft, but her kiss was fire—hot, desperate, claiming. The crowd's cheers reached a fever pitch. All I could hear was her sigh against my mouth, the faint hitch in her breath as she kissed me back. She was mine, and I was hers, and nothing else mattered.

We broke apart, our foreheads touching as we fought for breath. The announcer's voice boomed over the loudspeakers, declaring us the champions of the Sun and Moon Gauntlet. The crowd screamed our names in a hypnotic chant. It matched the beat of my heart, which had always whispered her name deep inside of me.

We turned to face the crowd, our hands clasped, waving as the cameras zoomed in on us. The crystal screens would be plastered with this moment, the kiss, the victory. They'd turn us into a story, a romance for the ages.

It was as we reached the edge of the stage that the reality crashed back in.

"Jorge? Is that…?"

I had known from the beginning that this wouldn't end well. I'd dared again to taste heaven. Once again, I'd been caught.

At night, my dreams were a fifty-fifty chance. Half the time I dreamt of Charlotte, holding her to me, kissing her wherever I could get my mouth on her. The other times, my lips split wide as I screamed while another woman took my hand.

Outside of the gates stood waiting the woman who had made me scream. My mechanical fingers wrapped around Charlotte's. The fingers holding hers weren't real, but my brain, my heart, processed it as real. I was so in tune with Charlotte that I sensed the sweat in her palms, the increase of her pulse as we looked at the mage who had torn us apart three years ago.

Unlike three years ago, Charlotte and I had a choice to make. The Convergence Games were held on sacred lands. Many countries warred on Lunaterra. But on this spot, even after the games were fought, any and all conflicts were null.

If we left, the mage had every right to take me into custody. I was in the army, the property of the crown.

If we stayed, then we both became the property of the Games and would have to fight again at the next event three years hence.

Three years.

Three years of nights with Charlotte in my arms.

Three years where no one and nothing could take her from me.

"Jorge, former second-in-command of the royal

army, you are hereby charged with deserting your post and making an attempt on the future queen's life."

"What?" Charlotte stepped forward, placing herself between me and the advancing guards. "That's absurd! I'm the future queen of Solmane. I am Princess Charlotte of Evergrove."

"A likely story, ma'am. The princess is safely in the care of the Prince Adom."

The look the mage gave Charlotte let the three of us know she knew exactly who Charlotte was. Instead of cutting off my hand this time, she was wrenching my heart from my body.

"Go, I will find you."

"No," Charlotte protested, holding me close. "Jorge, please. Please don't leave me again."

I pulled Charlotte to me and kissed her forehead. I only dared kiss the space between her head because I needed my wits about me. Anytime I tasted her breath or that sweet nectar between her thighs, I forgot I was mortal.

"Any parting between us is temporary," I swore.

"Don't you dare ask me to bear another second without you."

She slashed out with her blade. I would not have let her go. She could've gutted me in that moment and I would've asked if the cut was to her liking. But she pushed me away.

Her blade arced toward the guards, catching the first two who had advanced on us. Charlotte slashed again, her movements so fast, so fluid she had a clear shot at the mage.

The mage stepped back, but not before catching the tip of the blade on her forearm. I stepped between Charlotte and the three advancing guards, letting the blade taste my skin. With my body between Charlotte's and the guards, the men grabbed for me. The only reason they got me was because I let them.

I let them wrench my arms behind my back. I let them remove the blade at my side. I let them disarm me of my prosthetic.

"No!" Charlotte's scream tore through the air. The sound of it was sharp and biting, like a blade slicing through my chest.

One of the guards lunged for her.

Time slowed.

The prosthetic, still gripped in the hands of the guard who'd taken it, sprang to life. It twisted violently out of his grasp and launched itself at the throat of the guard advancing on Charlotte. The man staggered back, his hands clawing at his neck. Blood trickled where the edge of the blade had pressed against his skin.

"Touch her and die."

The guards froze, their gazes snapping to me. The

prosthetic hovered midair for a heartbeat longer before retreating, its blade retracting as it dropped politely back into the guard's hand. The man trembled, nearly dropping the appendage.

I turned to the mage, still holding her bloodied arm. My voice was steady and cold as ice. "I'll go quietly. But if anyone so much as lays a finger on a hair of her head —I will gut and quarter them. Do we understand each other?"

The mage said nothing but nodded her head.

The guards moved in, grabbing my arms and forcing me to my knees. The cold bite of steel shackles snapped around my wrists, the weight of them dragging against the phantom ache where my hand had once been.

I didn't feel a thing. Not in my arm. Not in my whole body.

CHAPTER EIGHTEEN

CHARLOTTE

My gaze was fixed on the iron gates of the prison as they slammed shut behind Jorge. The sound echoed in my chest like a death knell. I pressed my fingers against the carriage window, smudging the glass as I watched the guards shove him forward. He didn't resist, his broad shoulders slumped, his head bowed.

This was wrong. This wasn't how it was supposed to end. I turned to the mage, who was glaring at me. Before I opened my mouth, she answered my unasked question.

"His fate will be decided by Prince Adom. As commander of the military, it is his right to pass judgment."

Jorge had told me that he and the Beast Prince had fought side by side, that they'd even come to trust each other. But Jorge had also tried to steal his bride. Would Adom show mercy? Or would the beast let his claws do the talking?

"As for you, you will be returned to your employer. Belle, your name is? As the seamstress for the fairy princess, you must ensure her dress is ready for tomorrow's wedding."

"You know who I am."

The mage didn't deny it. Her silence spoke volumes, her expression one of knowing, like a predator waiting to strike.

"What do you want?"

The mage leaned back and regarded me as if amused by my defiance. "What I want is for you to understand your place in the scheme of the stars. My task is to ensure the curse is broken. That means the princess chosen by the first moon must marry the prince of Solmane."

"And if the princess refuses?"

The mage leaned forward until she was almost nose to nose with me. "The crown will make sure they break her toy soldier. And they'll send him back to her in pieces."

The mage made two mistakes. The first one was that she threatened Jorge's life. I had been calm while I'd thought they were just going to lock him up. The mention of ending his life meant all bets in whatever game she referred to were off.

The second mistake she made was that she let me get too close to her. There was an open wound on her arm from where I'd struck her. I grabbed hold of it and let my magic pour through.

Her eyes widened, and then she slumped down in the seat. She was completely numb from the top of her head down to the toes in her boots. She wouldn't be able to move for hours with as much of my magic as I pumped into her.

The carriage came to a stop inside the palace gates. I didn't wait for the driver to open the door. I climbed down, announcing that the mage had fallen asleep and I was headed back to my mistress. The driver didn't even question me.

Like the summer castle, once inside the walls of the palace, there were no guards. I knew the layout of the palace, including the rooms that would be mine. Looking the fright that I did, I knew I wouldn't make it past the servants in the main hall.

The door of the servants' entrance creaked as I slipped inside. The corridors were dark and silent. My footsteps were careful, measured, as I made my way to the second floor.

A cluster of guards was stationed at the next landing. There would be no sneaking past them. My gaze shifted to a nearby window, its frame just within reach. If going over walls had gotten me this far, I could climb farther.

The cool metal of the windowsill bit into my palms as I hoisted myself up and out. Outside, the wind whipped against my face, and I clung to the ledge for balance. My destination was clear: the grand window that opened into Prince Adom's chambers. If I could reach him, I could plead for Jorge's life. Beg if I had to.

The climb felt longer than it should have. Each pull of my arms reminded me of how my body ached from the gauntlet. My fingertips brushed the edge of the prince's window. When I reached for it, an invisible force repelled me.

I gasped, nearly losing my grip. A ward. Of course, he would ward his chambers.

I scanned the castle's exterior, my eyes catching on a smaller window glowing faintly with candlelight. If memory served, those were my quarters. Which meant Belle would be there, likely fussing over wedding preparations.

A new plan formed as I swung toward the glowing window, my muscles burning with the effort. When I reached it, the latch gave way under my hand, and I slipped inside.

The climb through the window had been the easy part—the landing, not so much. I tumbled through in a flurry of limbs and fabric, my gown catching on the frame with a sharp rip. Kicking free, I landed in a heap on the floor, gasping for air as though I'd just run a marathon.

"Charlotte?"

I collected myself and stood to face the seamstress. Instead of a hello, how are you, I lead with, "I need your help."

Belle gaped at me, scissors clutched in her hand like a sword. She pointed, the sharp tip shaking slightly. "You..."—she jabbed the air toward me—"...need my..." —she shifted the scissors toward herself—"...help?"

"Yes."

Her face turned crimson, and I braced myself for the outburst. "You ran away! You left me to marry the prince!"

"I never told you to marry the prince. That was your decision."

"Your decision left me with no choice! Your mother shoved a veil over my head and told me to go to him because you were gone. What was I supposed to do, say no to your mother?"

"I find it better to say nothing at all and then run."

Belle sputtered, words failing her. The wedding dress lay crumpled on the floor. It was beautiful—delicate embroidery shimmering in the candlelight, the fabric cascading like liquid gold. I picked it up, running my fingers over the intricate beading. "The dress came out nice."

"Nice?" Her voice dropped an octave, a low, furious growl. "Nice?"

"We don't have time for this. I need your help. It's about Jorge."

"Jorge? The human who tried to kidnap me?"

"He thought he was kidnapping me, not you. But it doesn't matter now. He's in trouble, and you're the only one who can get him out."

Her laugh was bitter. "You think I'm going to help you? After everything you've done?"

"Yes," I said simply, meeting her glare head-on. "You have to."

Belle scoffed, crossing her arms tighter, the scissors still clutched in her hand. "I don't have to do anything. You can't order me around anymore, Charlotte. I'm not your servant."

"You're not a princess, either."

"No, I'm nearly a queen."

We glared at each other. The charged silence crackled like static before a storm. One of us had to break first. I forced myself to soften, to let the storm clouds in my eyes dissolve. But not into rain. I couldn't let my defenses crack that much.

"Please, Belle. If you don't help me, Jorge will die."

So many emotions flittered over her face. I could see them being woven across her features. The finished creation somehow looked worn and tattered. "Fine, I'll help you."

Relief surged through me, but it was short-lived as her gaze hardened again.

"On one condition. You'll marry him; that's my condition."

I couldn't speak. The noose that had been around my neck since my birth tied itself into a new knot, one I didn't think I'd get out of a second time.

The moon hung low in the night sky. Avarix shone cold and distant, his pale light cutting through the shadows like a blade. It felt like he was glaring at me, judging me, punishing me. Avarix was supposed to protect us, to nurture the night-blooming flowers that sustained our people, but his light had grown dimmer with every passing year.

"Why wouldn't you want to be queen? You could have everything you've ever dreamed of—endless fabric to create your gowns. Or you wouldn't have to make gowns at all. You could wear them instead, show them off to the court."

"I don't want any of that, Charlotte." Belle sat down on the bed.

I slid down and sat beside her. "I don't want it either."

Jorge had once said Prince Adom had gotten under his skin, that they'd become friends despite everything. And now, looking at Belle, I saw that same bond reflected in her green eyes. Hopeless, doomed love. It wasn't fair. None of this was fair.

I turned to my could've-been-friend. "Why would you give him up if you love him?"

"You don't know about the curse, do you?"

"What curse?"

"Well, at least you're not as selfish as I thought." Belle pursed her lips as she apprised me anew. "His mother defied the moon and married the wrong man, and now he's cursed to live as a beast. Avarix will break the curse if he marries the fairy princess he choose for Adom: you."

"And if I don't?"

"If you don't marry him, the moon will take its revenge on Evergrove next."

CHAPTER NINETEEN

JORGE

$\mathcal{I}$ leaned back against the cold stone wall, my muscles aching from the rough treatment of the guards. I'd been stripped of everything, thrown into the dark like an animal. No, worse than an animal. At least they hadn't chained me. Yet.

My body was still, but my mind refused to rest. One thing I was certain of: this wasn't Adom's doing. The Lion Prince would've faced me directly, his claws bared, his amber eyes glaring into mine. Adom fought his battles with honor, no matter how much he despised the opponent.

No, this was the work of someone else. Someone more dangerous: the Sky Keeper Mages. They didn't care about honor. Only outcomes.

I flexed the fingers of my remaining hand, the muscles in my arm twitching at the absence of weight on the other side. I felt the phantom of it, the mech I'd built and rebuilt over the years, as much a part of me as my own flesh and bone. They could strip it from my body, but not my mind. I was still linked to it, still in it.

I slowed my breathing, letting my heart rate even out. The coldness of the cell began to fade as I sank into my focus. The faint hum of energy that connected me to the prosthetic sparked to life. My awareness spread outward, beyond the confines of the cell. Past the bars. Past the guards who had sneered at me as they hauled me in. The prosthetic wasn't far—it couldn't be. I searched for it in the dark, the pulse of my connection stretching like a hand reaching through shadows.

There.

The faint flicker of power hummed at the edge of my consciousness, the metal fingers twitching where they'd discarded it. They'd left it among the rubble, assuming it was nothing more than a glorified decoration without me attached to it. Fools.

I brought it back online with a thought. A rush of relief flooded through me as I felt it respond, as though a part of me had just taken its first breath after being suffocated. My next move was already forming in my mind when the sound of approaching footsteps broke my concentration.

Boots. Two sets. One heavy and deliberate, the other light and cautious. The clink of keys on a ring accompanied their approach. The light from a flickering torch danced off the damp walls, casting long, distorted shadows that grew closer with each second.

I pulled myself back into my body but kept my form limp against the wall. I was the picture of dejection and rejection. It was an easy role to play. I had tons of first-hand material to act it out.

The flowery scent hit me and knocked my spine up straight. The fragrance was too delicate for this place. It clung to the air, sweet and unmistakably fairy.

Charlotte.

No. Wait. It was too sweet. No sharp tang of embers coating it.

Even cloaked in shadows, the imposter wore her resemblance like a weapon. Her lavender skin, her curls, even the tilt of her head mimicked Charlotte perfectly.

The guard unlocked the door. The imposter—Belle, her name came to me like a whisper—took a step forward, then hesitated. Her hands hovered near me as if she wanted to help but didn't dare.

Smart girl.

I stumbled toward her, each step calculated agony. When I got close enough, I noticed something that made my gut twist. She was wearing Charlotte's cloak. Had Charlotte given it to her? Or had Belle taken it from her cold, dead body? I was certain I knew the answer.

Outside, sunlight seared my eyes. The partial eclipse cast eerie shadows across the ground. The light filtered through Avarix's shadowed ring, dim yet piercing. Belle handed me my prosthetic, and I set about reassembling myself.

"Let me guess; she traded herself for my freedom."

Belle flinched but nodded, unable to meet my gaze.

"And you agreed, because you love him."

Her silence was confirmation enough.

A laugh escaped me, sharp and humorless. "I had every plan to kill that bastard, but he got under my skin, too."

"Adom acts like he's a monster. But he's really just a cub who wants to cuddle."

That pulled a real laugh from me. "I'm sure he'll love hearing that from the woman he loves."

She turned to me, surprise flashing in her green eyes. For a moment, we shared a strange sort of camaraderie. Two people bound by impossible choices and the love of people who'd never truly be ours.

Then the wedding bells tolled, breaking the moment.

I didn't move. I sank onto a nearby rock, my body screaming in protest, and stared toward the distant palace. Ten minutes passed in silence, each second dragging like an eternity. The bells rang again, their tone brighter, announcing the vows had been said.

It was done. Charlotte was married. She'd said the vows to another man. It was lies, but it was a contract that couldn't be undone.

Then the roar came.

It wasn't a sound—it was a force, shaking the ground and reverberating through the city like a shockwave. Raw and guttural, it carried rage and heartbreak. I didn't need to see who it belonged to. I knew.

Belle and I exchanged a glance. Before we could move, the air shifted. Guards poured in from every direction, their armor gleaming even in the dim eclipse light. Not mage guards, not shifters—fae.

They knocked Belle out with barely a tap to the back of her head. She wasn't a fighter. She'd screamed like a damsel back at the summer castle. If I'd had Charlotte at my side, I might have made it out of this.

The guards at the prison just watched. I wasn't their problem any longer.

"The queen wants a word with you."

CHAPTER TWENTY

CHARLOTTE

The silk of the gown pooled around me in decadent waves, the fabric so delicate it felt like I could dissolve into it. My fingers traced the intricate embroidery along the bodice—Belle's handiwork, every stitch a masterpiece. She had been right. It was beautiful. The kind of gown meant for a fairy princess, meant to be admired, envied, worshipped.

All eyes had been on me. Too bad the only pair of eyes I'd wanted to see hadn't been there.

I had whispered my vows with my eyes closed beneath the veil, pretending it was him standing before me. I had spoken words of devotion, of duty, of forever, and I had meant every single one of them—not for the Beast Prince, but for the man who had held my heart long before I ever knew what love was.

But then the veil had lifted.

Prince Adom's sharp eyes had met mine, and in that moment, the fury that should have ignited never came. Instead, his face slackened, his pupils dilating. His lips parted, as if he meant to speak, but then—he wavered. He collapsed. Then he shifted.

The man in the bed was no beast. He was unfairly handsome. His features were sharp, regal, as if the gods had sculpted him with a perfection meant to frustrate artists. As a beast, he had been fierce and commanding; as a man, he was a vision.

But not my vision.

He was not Jorge.

And yet I'd bound myself to him.

How could I do this? How could I go another three minutes, let alone three years, without his face, his touch, his voice murmuring my name like it was sacred?

My grip tightened on the dagger. I wasn't going to stay. I couldn't.

I'd said the vows. The curse was broken. The beast was human. The moon was appeased. There was no edict that I had to stay. But escaping wouldn't be easy.

The Beast Prince stirred. Though perhaps I shouldn't call him that any longer. Since he was human.

Prince Adom stirred, his golden lashes fluttering as he opened his eyes. He stared blankly at the ceiling, his face slack with confusion. Then he sat up and swung his legs off the bed. His movements were unhurried, as though he'd woken in a stranger's body. His gaze landed on the mirror across the room, and he rose, stalking toward it.

He stood before the mirror, studying himself. Was it vanity? Or disbelief? His fingers brushed over his jaw, his reflection's smooth, unmarred skin where once fur and claws had ruled. He turned sharply, finally noticing me in the room.

"Hi, I'm Charlotte. Your wife."

"I'm Adom. Your husband."

We stood in silence, appraising each other like adversaries rather than partners. He sank heavily onto the bed, running a hand through his wild mane of hair. I hesitated, then joined him, careful to keep space between us.

"Are you planning to use that?" he asked, nodding at the dagger still twirling between my fingers.

I caught it mid-spin and studied its glinting edge. "It's beautiful, isn't it? Jorge made it for me. For my twelfth birthday."

"He was planning to rescue you. Not her."

I nodded, the truth settling heavily between us.

"Where is she?"

"I don't know."

He rose and crossed to the door, testing it. Locked. Of course it was.

"We're under orders from the Sky Keeper Mages to finish the marriage ritual before they'll let us out."

"Finish?" His tone was flat, though the glint in his eye suggested he already understood.

"You know…" I motioned toward the rumpled sheets, still untouched on the side he hadn't slept on.

His shoulders tensed. He looked so disturbed, as though the very thought of being violated—of being at someone else's mercy—was a wound too deep to articulate. I was surprised he didn't clutch for imaginary pearls around his neck.

"I didn't touch you while you were sleeping. Even though my consent was taken from me on the day I was born, I wasn't going to take yours from you."

"But you were going to give yourself to me, to this union?"

"No. I wasn't planning to stay long."

"Jorge is waiting for you somewhere?"

"You didn't have him taken?"

"I have no idea where he went after he tried to steal her."

"Then she must have him," I muttered, the pieces clicking into place. "She'll kill him this time."

I kicked the door in frustration. It shuddered under the force but didn't budge. Panic clawed at my chest, hot and suffocating. "If she has Jorge, she'll have Belle too."

Adom's head tilted, his eyes narrowing. "Who's…"

"I ran from you at the Summer Castle, and Belle was forced by my mother to take my place. Belle and I traded places last night. She went to save Jorge in exchange for me taking my place and marrying you so that I could break the curse."

Prince Adom's jaw tightened, the golden hue in his eyes deepening. A low rumble started in his chest, the lion within him waking to find itself caged in a human body.

"Belle wanted to marry you. I think she actually loves you. But she knew she couldn't break the curse. And I had to save Jorge. I love him with all of my heart, and I won't let her take him away from me again. He's mine."

Adom's exhale vibrated in the air between us, low and primal, carrying with it a weight that pressed against my chest. His golden eyes flickered, molten and alive, glowing brighter than they should in the dim light of the chamber. The rumble in his chest grew louder, deeper, shaking the floor beneath my feet.

I took an involuntary step back, the dagger still clutched in my hand. "Adom?"

He didn't answer. His body visibly tensed as though something inside him was clawing to get free. His muscles rippled beneath his skin. The lines of his face sharpened, becoming more feral. His hands clenched at his sides. The tendons in his neck stood out in stark relief.

Then he growled—a sound so raw and guttural it made me clutch my blade for protection. The room shrank around him as his form shifted. His shoulders broadened, his limbs lengthened, his fingers curled into claws that gleamed like obsidian.

He bent forward, his back arching. Bones snapped and realigned, the sound reverberating through the chamber. His mane of golden hair grew wilder, spilling down his back in waves that caught the faint light. His face elongated, the regal features of a man morphing into the commanding visage of a lion. A thick tail lashed behind him, brushing against the floor with a low, threatening hiss.

The transformation was as terrifying as it was magnificent. His clothes tore at the seams, falling away in shreds as fur overtook his body, rich and golden like the fields at dusk. His paws hit the floor with a heavy thud, claws raking the stone as he straightened to his full height.

His glowing eyes met mine. I saw the man behind the beast. There was pain there. There was also rage behind those molten gold irises.

Prince Adom broke the door down with his front paws. Screams erupted from outside. Then he turned and made a motion with his head. I didn't speak lion, but I got his message. I hopped on his back, still clothed in my wedding dress, and hung on to his mane for dear life.

CHAPTER TWENTY-ONE

JORGE

The shackles weighed heavily on my wrists, biting into the raw skin beneath. The royal guard had coated the shackles in a nullifying alloy. It was one I had created. Unfortunately, I hadn't bothered to develop a counter against this counter attack. I'd never expected my own creation would be used on me.

Every jolt of the carriage sent a fresh wave of pain up my arms and across my back. My body screamed in protest. I bit down on the agony. Pain was an old friend. It had walked beside me in the stables, in the games, in the barracks, and now in the rattling dark of this cursed wagon.

The carriage ground to a halt, the wooden wheels creaking against the gravel road. My ears perked at the sound of another set of wheels coming to rest nearby. Through the small, barred window, I caught a glimpse of the royal crest embossed on a carriage gilded in gold.

I braced myself, imagining the Beast Prince's claws around my throat. But when the door to the royal carriage swung open, it wasn't Adom who descended.

Her golden eyes scanned her surroundings with predatory precision. Her mane of sunlit hair caught the light like a halo, though there was nothing angelic about the Lioness Queen.

The guards dragged Belle's limp body from the carriage like a sack of flour. Once again, I marveled that anyone could confuse her and my Charlotte. She was so small, so still where Charlotte would've been kicking and screaming. Even still, Belle hadn't deserved any of this.

"Take her inside," the Lioness Queen ordered.

The guards obeyed without hesitation, carrying Belle into the palace as though the weight of her body didn't matter. The Lioness turned, her golden eyes locking on me like I was a foal cut off from the herd.

"You were his friend."

"I am his friend."

The queen's lips curved into something between a frown and a sneer. "And yet you stole his bride."

"Charlotte is my world." My voice gained strength with every word. "My heart is hers to command. As long as she wants me, I'll fight to get back to her."

"He won't be fighting much longer." The Fairy Queen appeared, her lavender skin shimmering under the light of the two suns. Her eyes glinted with malice as she glared at me.

The Lioness Queen didn't acknowledge her immediately. She kept her gaze fixed on me, her expression unreadable. Finally, she spoke, her voice low and deliberate. "You would betray your future king, your country, for that fairy?"

"Yes, Your Majesty. The late king was your great love. What if you had been told to marry someone else instead of him? Would you have done the same?"

Her lips twitched in the ghost of a smile, but it didn't reach her eyes. "It was a dangerous game you attempted to play. Attempted and lost."

"Who exactly lost?"

She studied me for another moment. "I pray she grants you a quick death. We should all be so lucky."

"I wish I could kill him now and be done with it," the Fairy Queen hissed in frustration, her delicate features twisting in fury. "I have to return to Evergrove. A mother's work is never done. Is it, Amara?"

"It's Your Majesty." The Lioness Queen corrected the Fairy Queen without so much as a glance her way.

The Fairy Queen's smirk faltered, the edges of her carefully composed expression cracking like fragile porcelain. Her eyes darted away from the queen's and met with mine.

"You were never a mother to her," I snarled. "You were a madam."

Queen Indira snapped her fingers at the guards, her voice dripping with venom. "Make it slow. Make it agonizing. And leave the body for the trolls."

The carriage lurched forward again, this time taking flight. The pegasuses' wings beat heavily against the air. Their gait was uneven beneath us. Something was wrong.

The carriage swayed unnaturally. The wheels clattered every so often, as if they scraped against an uneven track. But we were in the air, not on the ground. We weren't going to get far, and when we landed, I'd be ready.

But ready for what? To go back to the capitol and save Charlotte? Was I really saving her? What would life with me even look like? Living in barns? Fighting for our lives as the royal army chased after us?

Maybe if I left her with Adom, she would be fine. Adom wasn't a bad man, far from it. He was one of the best men I knew.

The problem was that he didn't have the capacity to make Charlotte happy. I couldn't stand by and watch her live an unhappy life. That just wasn't in me.

The wind roared past us as the pegasus soared higher into the evening sky. Beneath us, the rolling hills of Solmane blurred into shadowy streaks. Every muscle in my body ached from the awkward position I was bound in. I ignored the pain and began to work on my binds. There had to be a way out of them.

"Something's wrong with the steeds," one of the guards barked over the rush of wind.

I craned my neck, squinting against the blinding speed as I tried to catch sight of the problem. A series of jerky movements rippled through the pegasus herd. Their harnesses creaked ominously. The metal clasps strained against the force of the flight. One of the beasts emitted a distressed cry, its shimmering wings faltering before resuming their rhythm. I felt the uneasy shift in our altitude, the way the steed carrying us wobbled slightly.

"He's good with beasts," another guard shouted. "I remember him from the village. He can fix it."

"We're supposed to kill him, not give him busywork."

"If he fixes the wing, we can offer to make it a quick death," the second one countered, his tone laced with practicality. "It'll save the lot of us from a crash."

The first guard hesitated, grumbling under his breath. Finally, he shouted, "Fine. Let's set them down and make him fix it quick."

"Put her down over there. There's a blacksmith in that village. He'll have the tools we need."

We descended abruptly. Dust billowed around us as the carriage settled to the ground. The herd walked the rest of the way to the forge. The familiar sound of hammering reached my ears, the unmistakable rhythm of a blacksmith at work.

I was dragged from the carriage. I focused, letting my body go limp to make the guards think I was giving in. They grunted in frustration as they adjusted their hold. Good. The less they watched my hands, the better.

The alloy might have locked the larger mechanisms, but it couldn't smother the micro-pulses in the finger-tips. Those circuits weren't made to power brute strength. They were made for precision. And precision was all I needed.

"Oy!" the guard called to the figures emerging from the forge. "We need some tools to fix our herd. We'll pay."

"You can take all the tools you want if you leave us him."

It was a voice I hadn't heard in years but had never truly escaped. A voice that had haunted my nights in the stables, shouted commands I couldn't refuse, and spat insults that had taken root deep in my chest.

My knees truly did give out then. My hands were free of the shackles. But they dangled uselessly at my side. My mind screamed at me to run, to fight, to do something, but my body refused to move.

The years I'd spent clawing my way out of their shadows, building myself into someone stronger, someone untouchable—it all crumbled in an instant. My chest tightened, the air growing thin as hopelessness settled over me like a suffocating shroud.

I thought I'd buried this part of my life. I thought I'd left them behind in the ashes of my past. Seeing them now, I was that skinny, weak boy again, trembling under their fists and their jeers.

Uncle Maris' smile widened, full of malice and triumph. "Did you miss us, boy?" he sneered, stepping closer. "Don't worry. We'll make you feel right at home."

I couldn't breathe. I couldn't think. All I could do was watch as the shadows of my past closed in, and for the first time in years, I felt utterly, irreparably lost.

CHAPTER TWENTY-TWO

CHARLOTTE

The pegasus's hooves pounded against the air as I leaned low over its neck, urging it faster. The wind screamed past me, whipping my hair into a wild, tangled halo. The familiar rolling hills of Evergrove came into view, their moonlit beauty tainted by the storm in my chest. The scent of nightblooming jasmine filled the air, but it wasn't enough to soothe me. Not tonight.

Adom had lent me his fastest steed from the summer castle's stables after we'd found Belle wandering in the forests, intent on saving Adom from a loveless marriage with me. To her delight, she'd learned that her vows to the prince when they'd consummated their relationship the night before superseded any deals we'd made. She and Adom belonged together. Now I just needed to rescue the man who was mine.

If only this pegasus would fly faster. I knew my mother's intentions. If I didn't get there five minutes ago, an hour ago, it might be too late.

The stables came into view first. I leaped off the steed before all four hooves had made impact. I pushed open the doors of the stables. The emptiness inside felt like a physical blow. The place where Jorge's forge once roared was cold and abandoned, its tools neatly stacked but untouched. The straw bed where we'd spent stolen moments together was clean, devoid of any sign that he'd ever been here.

No one had worked here since he left. We hadn't had the money to hire anyone to work for free. The only way we'd survived these last three years was because the Moonkeepers had kept us under guard. They were all gone now that their mission had been fulfilled.

The Beast Prince was wed. And to the right woman. Adom's vows to Belle had broken the curse. I was free to return to the promise I'd made Jorge when we were too young to understand what our vows to each other meant. I just had to find him.

My feet carried me to the manor before my mind could catch up. The grand doors loomed ahead, carved with intricate patterns that spoke of a time when Evergrove was wealthy and thriving. Now the wood was weathered, the edges frayed with neglect. I shoved the doors open, letting them crash against the walls as I stormed into the foyer.

Queen Indira stood in the sitting room, draped in silks and jewels. Her face was a mask of cold composure. Her gaze flicked up to meet mine. A smile that didn't reach her eyes curled her lips.

"Charlotte, what are you doing here? You're getting coronated in the morning."

"Where is he?" I strode toward her, my dagger clutched tightly in my hand.

"You need to get back before he realizes you're gone. You don't want to upset the Beast."

"His name is Adom—King Adom—and he sent me here to find his second in command. You know him as Jorge."

Queen Indira arched an elegant brow, as if I were a petulant child throwing a tantrum. "Why should I know where your little human pet is?"

"Do not play games with me, Mother. The blood of the last person who tried to play me is still on my blade. The Lioness Queen told Belle she gave him to you."

"That bitch. She won't renege on our deal."

"That's truly all you care about, isn't it? The money. Your status."

"What else is there?"

"Love."

"Don't be childish, girl. Try eating love."

"Where is he?" I shouted.

"He's not here."

"Tell me where he is." I pressed the dagger against her mute lips. "I won't let you kill Jorge because he dared to love me."

"Wrong tense, darling. I'm not going to kill Jorge."

My heart lightened. I lowered the blade.

"He's already dead."

It wasn't true. It couldn't be true. My heart still beat. So he was still in this world. But just to be sure, I pressed my dagger to my mother's throat.

"You've been lying to me my entire life. You said I was chosen by the moon, that my marriage to the Beast Prince would save Evergrove. But it was the moon that cursed him. And it was the suns that blessed Belle and Adom. Lyra blessed them because they love each other, and she prized that. Which means the moon no longer has an interest in me. Which means I can have my love, finally. So you tell me where he is."

I raised the dagger, my aim true. The blade caught the moonlight streaming through the windows. Gasps echoed from the gathered servants and courtiers who had crept into the edges of the room to watch the confrontation unfold. The fear in my mother's eyes was palpable, and for the first time in my life, I felt like I had power over her.

"Give him back to me."

The queen's lips trembled, and for a moment, I thought she might beg. More the fool was I.

Queen Indira straightened, her chin lifting. "It's too late. He's gone."

"He's not gone. I would feel it. I would know."

My chest heaved, my thoughts a whirlwind of rage and despair. I could kill her. It would be so easy. One quick thrust, and all her lies, all her manipulations, would die with her.

"I told them to make him suffer and put the body where the trolls would find him."

A sob escaped my lips. A trickle of blood escaped a thin cut at my mother's neck. I stared at the red. It entranced me. I wanted more of it.

"Take her," called my mother. "Take her."

People burst into the room. But these weren't the Moonkeepers. These were the fae servants who had remained—those who had endured years of my mother's mistreatment and watched as she squandered their lands and lives. One by one, they moved to stand behind me. Their allegiance was clear. This wasn't just my rebellion—it was theirs, too.

"You wish us to take her to the dowager house, Your Grace?"

"The dowager house?" My mother's nose wrinkled in disgust.

The dowager house was nothing like the summer palace that the Lioness Queen would retire to now that her son had taken the crown. The dowager house was a two-bedroom shack without indoor plumbing. Or what my mother would call a living hell.

"No. Give her a carriage, a gredane to pull it, and cast her out in the street to make her way in the world."

The servants looked hesitant. They had spent years under her rule and my silence. They would do well to send us both out into the world in a rickety carriage with only one slow beast to carry our load. Goddess knows I never did anything to lighten any of their loads or make their lives better. I'd only cared about one other person my whole life. And it wasn't the prince I'd been groomed for. It was the groom who came to rule my heart.

A heavy silence settled over the hall, thick with uncertainty. The servants—men and women who had bowed to my mother's whims for years—shifted uneasily, glancing between us, weighing their loyalty.

Would they see me as their salvation? Or just another queen, cut from the same cloth?

CHAPTER TWENTY-THREE

JORGE

"Move, you lazy beast."

I didn't jolt out of my stupor when Uncle Maris snapped at me. I was stuck inside the anticipation, waiting for the pain. I didn't wait long. The slap… it barely registered.

His hand, once a thing of brute force, was nothing more than a brittle relic of my past nightmares. His fingers, gnarled and twisted from years of labor and age, could barely extend fully. The strike was weak, a ghost of the blows that used to send me reeling. It carried no weight, no real sting—just the memory of a frail, unloved boy who had cowered under this man's shadow.

I wasn't that boy anymore.

I was a soldier, a warrior, a man who had fought and bled for his place in the world. A man who had the love of a princess, the respect of a kingdom, and a strength Uncle Maris could never touch.

He couldn't hurt me now. Not with his words, not with his hands.

He raised his hand again. I watch that gnarled thing come toward me. I had no interest in being struck. So I don't get struck. I shifted, so he hit air and tumbled forward.

My cousins looked murderous. But it was the guards who were smarter. They charged me. They knew it was me or them. My family hadn't a clue who they were dealing with. My cousins were too busy helping their father to his feet.

My blade extended with a whisper of steel. A sharp gasp escaped the first guard before he crumpled to the ground. The second guard was only just turning when I lunged, my prosthetic arm slamming into his chest with a force that sent him staggering back. The blade found its mark, and he slumped into the dirt beside his partner, the life draining from his eyes.

I wasn't even out of breath. I bent down to clean my blade on their clothing, giving my family my back. It was the ultimate show of disrespect when a warrior presents his vulnerable side to his enemy.

"Now you've done it, boy. Those were fae guards. You think your little flower skirt will get you out of a murder charge?"

Did everyone know about Charlotte and my affair? We'd thought we hid it so well.

"We should grab him. Might be a reward for turning in a killer." That was Olric's voice. "Grab the little crackling, Dain."

There was a dull thud and the sound of rocks kicked as boots stumbled forward and halted. The blood cleaned from my blade, I rose to my full height and turned to face them.

Dain was a step ahead of the other two males. He quickly stepped back. Olric clung to his father in what could be mistaken as a show of holding the old man up. But the way Olric's fingers curled into his father's shirt-sleeves gave away his cowardice.

There was fear in their faces. I drank it in like a man starved for justice. Caution clung to the deep grooves etched into their overworked, malnourished faces, settling in the hollows of their gaunt cheeks and the nervous twitch of their hands. Their once-imposing frames, the ones that had towered over me in my youth, were now brittle with age and hardship. Their skin had taken on a sallow, sunken quality, stretched too tight over bones that no longer carried strength.

Once, they had been giants in my eyes, their presence casting long, suffocating shadows over my childhood. But now, stripped of the power they'd once wielded over me, they were nothing more than broken things—hollow and shrunken, their edges dulled by the same cruelty they had inflicted on others. But then their fear hardened into something uglier—resentment, bolstered by years of misplaced pride.

My uncle was the first to recover, his lips curling into a sneer. "You always were a freak, Jorge."

Olric gripped a hammer so tightly his knuckles turned white, while Dain shifted uneasily, clearly wishing he were anywhere else. Once, they'd towered over me, their laughter cruel and their blows merciless. They'd been my tormentors, thriving on my weakness. But now… now I saw them for what they truly were.

Pathetic. Petty. Cowards.

The corner of my mouth twitched, but I didn't smile. Instead, I lowered my blade and stood tall, letting them see me, all of me—scarred, enhanced, and unbreakable. My posture dared them to come at me.

No one moved.

"You're nothing." My uncle spat on the ground. "Always have been. Always will be."

Olric swung the hammer in a nervous arc, as if testing its weight.

Dain muttered something under his breath, too low for me to catch.

I didn't care. They could call me whatever they wanted. Their words couldn't reach me anymore. I turned my back to them and walked away.

"Crackling coward."

I had no idea which one of them bellowed that at my back. Their voices sounded the same as the insults came fast and thick. I kept walking, every muscle in my body ready to react should one of them try to strike.

Their voices grew louder, desperate to reclaim some semblance of power. I could hear it in the pitch of their taunts, the rising hysteria. They needed me to react, needed me to turn and engage.

Something whistled through the air.

I didn't need to turn to know what it was. Metal had always spoken to me. I could feel the weight of it, the shape, the familiarity of its build. A hammer was airborne and aimed for the back of my skull.

I lifted my prosthetic arm, aiming without turning. A pulse of energy surged through the plating, gears shifting into place as I unleashed the blast.

The hammer never reached me.

The shockwave met it midair, sending it hurtling backward like a comet returning to its maker. It struck the forge with a deafening crack, colliding with the roof before bouncing into the piles of wood and scattered embers. A hiss filled the air as the first flames licked hungrily at the dry beams.

Maris cursed. Olric and Dain scrambled, their heavy footfalls shifting from pursuit to panic. The thick smoke curled into the air. The heat licked at my back.

I didn't stop.

Didn't turn.

Didn't spare them so much as a glance.

Their fate wasn't mine to hold.

They had made their bed in cinders. Let them lie in it. The past was ash, and I wasn't staying to breathe it in.

I wasn't the broken boy they'd once beaten into submission. I was a survivor. A fighter. And I had someone to fight for.

I picked up my pace. Charlotte was my future, my everything. And no one—not my family, not prince or queen, not even the gods themselves—would keep me from her.

I needed to get back to the capital. But I couldn't walk. I needed a functioning ride or a fast ley line. The closest was in Evergrove.

CHAPTER TWENTY-FOUR

CHARLOTTE

"I left to wed the Prince of Solmane, only to finally realize that I am a princess of Evergrove."

I stood before the gathered crowd in a simple dress. I'd almost come out in leathers but thought that would be too much on this, my first address as their queen. The gathered crowd—nobles in embroidered silks, merchants in practical wool cloaks, commoners in work-worn linen—stood in wary silence.

They didn't trust me.

Why should they?

I had been a ghost in my own home, a princess who never looked beyond the gilded walls of the manor to see the toil of the merchant class, who dined among the nobility but never truly saw them, who passed the servants in the halls without knowing their names or the burdens they carried.

They had all been shadows at the edges of my world, faceless and voiceless. I had never asked about their lives, never wondered what dreams they held or what struggles they endured beneath my mother's rule. I had been wrapped in silks and expectations, my world no larger than the path laid out before me. I had let my mother's reign crush them beneath debt and neglect, just as she had tried to do to me.

"I renounced the throne of Solmane."

That got a rise out of them.

The nobles clutched at their chests, their fingers curling possessively around jeweled brooches and golden chains, as if my words might somehow strip them of their wealth and privilege. There was a collective sigh through the merchant class ranks. The sound carried the weight of fatigue rather than shock. Their hands twitched as though already tallying the cost of this shift in power, calculating what it would mean for their stalls, their trade routes, their profit margins.

The servants, however, were still as stone, their spines stiff with the quiet endurance of those who had seen rulers come and go while they always remained at the bottom. What difference did it make who sat in the manor if they would still rise before dawn, still serve the same meals, still bow and scrape and fade into the background?

"Some may say Avarix will punish us because I didn't make the vow he demanded. It was the Mother Sun and the Daughter Moon that blessed King Adom's union with one of our own. It is the suns that shine their light on Evergrove and will return us to prosperity."

The sky above was no longer veiled in shadow. The eclipse was over. Lyra's light dominated the heavens. Avarix hovered faintly in the distance, a pale remnant of the night, but it felt weak—diminished. Good. Avarix had never been a friend to me. His cold light cast judgment over every misstep I'd ever made. I wouldn't bow to him, not now, not ever.

Lyra burned bright, defiant against her mother's dominance. I found a kinship in her light. She refused to be overshadowed, to be silenced, to be ruled by a mother who only cared for her light. I whispered a silent promise to myself: *Neither will I.*

Jorge had been my Lyra, fierce and unwavering. But he'd also been my Solara, selfless and giving, protecting me even when I didn't deserve it. He never asked for my compliance, never demanded that I shape myself to fit his desires. He would have died for me—might already have. That thought struck me like a blade. I clenched my fists, my nails biting into my palms. I couldn't let it end like this.

"We have the tools we need to rebuild, to grow stronger. And many of those tools came from someone who wasn't even one of us. A human. Jorge.

"Jorge didn't just survive in Evergrove—he thrived. He found ways to coat metals so they wouldn't harm us. He cared for our animals, ensuring their strength and health. He created nighttime irrigation to help our crops bloom when Avarix's light failed us.

"Jorge was taken from us three years ago. But he didn't stop fighting. He fought his way out of the Convergence Games. He fought for us in the Troll Wars to become the second commander to King Adom. He has always fought for us. Now I'm going to fight for him, and when I find him, he will be your king."

Another murmur went through the crowd. Some fairies bristled. Some nodded their assent. There was no overwhelming consensus of my declaration for Jorge's role in this society. We wouldn't have a smooth way, but nothing had been easy about our love since its beginning. What were a few more ruffled wings?

"I'll need help finding him and for the fight that will ensue. Who's with me?"

"I'll go with you."

His voice cut through the crowd like a blade, slicing through every worry, every plan, every stubborn wall I had built to hold myself together. My spine locked, my grip tightening around the dagger at my side. The sunlight caught the steel, but I could barely see it. My vision blurred, my ears rang, my pulse roared.

I turned, frantically searching the sea of faces, desperate and terrified all at once. And then—I saw it.

A hand rose above the crowd. Not flesh and bone, but metal and power.

A sob tore from my throat, raw and unbidden, and I couldn't stop it, couldn't contain the flood of emotion that crashed over me.

Jorge stood there, grinning, as if the last three years had never happened. As if he hadn't been ripped from me three days ago, hadn't been thrown into hell, hadn't fought and bled and clawed his way back to me.

"Or we can stay, and you can come here into my arms where you belong."

I didn't think.

I ran.

CHAPTER TWENTY-FIVE

JORGE

Charlotte crashed into me. I caught her as if I'd been waiting my whole life to do just that. Because I had.

She felt exactly as she should—like warmth, like home, like a part of me. I buried my face against her neck, breathing her in. The scent of crushed petals and battle-sweat settled into my bones.

She was here. In my arms. And I would never let her go.

Then a whisper. Low at first, but growing. The sound of shifting weight, of murmured dissent. A voice finally rose above the rest, its tone dripping with disdain.

"She can't expect us to bow down to a human."

I'd known it wouldn't be easy. I'd spent years plotting, scheming, fighting just to be near Charlotte again, let alone stand at her side in the open. And now, as her people—our people—watched with wary eyes, doubt and judgment swirling among them, I realized something.

I was done hiding.

I was done waiting.

I would not scheme or crawl or pretend I was anything less than what I was: a man who loved her. A man who had fought through blood and fire to stand beside her.

I began to set her on her feet, ready to step forward and face the challenge head-on.

Charlotte beat me to it.

Steel flashed.

The noble fae male barely had time to react before Charlotte's dagger was pressed to his throat.

"I may not be a money-grubbing, social-climbing snake like my mother." The snarl curled from her lips, carrying through the crowd. "But I am a warrior, and I will gut anyone who comes for what is mine."

The fae male swallowed hard, his throat bobbing against the blade.

"Make no mistake that I protect what is mine. The man who has my heart as well as the people under my care. Stay under my rule or leave now. Those are your choices."

Silence. Heavy. Unrelenting.

Charlotte pulled the dagger away, stepping back. Before she could say another word, I grabbed her wrist. I yanked her to me. And then I kissed her.

Right there, before them all. I kissed her slow, deep, and claiming.

The merchants chuckled, murmuring approval. The servants whooped, delighted. The nobles? The nobles still looked uneasy.

I grinned against Charlotte's lips. We'd manage them later. Right now, there was a more pressing matter. It was pressing hard against the front of my pants into Charlotte's belly.

I don't remember leaving the town square. Sometime later, we arrived at the path that led to the manor. I'd come to this place twelve years ago, not realizing it would be the one place in the world that I would find love and acceptance.

As the grand edifice of the manor loomed before us, I felt Charlotte's hand in mine, her grip firm and assertive. She had always been the flame to my moth. Any time spent away from her had been nothing but darkness—a vast, empty night where the cold gnawed at my bones and every breath felt hollow.

With her, there was light. There was warmth. She burned bright enough to chase away the shadows that had haunted me for years, and I would follow her into the fire without hesitation, even if it consumed me whole.

She tugged me toward the manor instead of the stables, and my steps faltered.

"No more sneaking around in stables. Well, not unless we're role-playing. You're the master of the house now. We'll fuck in the master suite."

We stepped inside, the heavy wooden door closing behind us with a resonant thud. The familiar faces of the servants greeted us. Their features were expression-less, but there was still a knowing as they bowed their heads in respectful acknowledgment.

The moment the door to the master suite clicked shut behind us, Charlotte's fingers tore at the buttons of her gown. The material parted, revealing swathes of pale purple skin that drank in the daylight.

I had only ever seen her body by candlelight, in the dead of night. Her wings, the pride of her fae heritage, unfolded with a whisper of dark purple elegance. She stretched them wide, the delicate membrane fluttering like the petals of a night-blooming flower. My mouth watered like a faucet turned on full blast. There was the sight of her bared breasts, the ripe swell of desire between her legs, and those magnificent wings making my cock even harder.

I shed my clothes in haste, discarding them without care as my gaze remained locked on the vision before me. The distance between us vanished as she reached out, her hands finding purchase on my shoulders and pulling me down onto the bed atop her waiting form.

"Let me taste you, starlight."

"Not this time. I want you inside me first."

With a lithe twist of her hips, Charlotte flipped us. Now atop me, she positioned herself, her fingers circling the base of my arousal. A languid smile played on her lips as she guided me to her entrance, and then, with a single fluid motion, she descended upon me.

As Charlotte took control, riding me with an insatiable rhythm, I let her. She was always welcome to have her way with me. It was just the way the gods made me.

My hands roamed over the silken expanse of her purple skin, tracing the contours that I knew so well yet could never tire of exploring. Her wings quivered with each thrust and swivel of her hips.

I gritted my teeth, fighting to hold back the tide of pleasure threatening to overwhelm me. Her body enveloped me completely. The sensation of her working me, sliding up and down, sent shivers through my thighs on down to my toes.

Her pace quickened, breaths coming in short gasps, signaling the approach of her release. With a sudden arch of her back, Charlotte's climax tore through her. Her inner muscles clenched tightly, milking me with a fervor that pushed me past the brink.

My patience was no match for the tight sleeve of her intimate muscles. I came at the first involuntary clench. The feeling I'd had on my tongue, on my fingers, was multiplied immeasurably with her muscles squeezing the life out of my cock. Together, we crested the wave of ecstasy, our cries mingling in the air.

Spent from the force of her orgasm, Charlotte's strength waned. She collapsed down onto me, a cascade of dark purple tresses framing her flushed face. Her weight was a welcome comfort, grounding me as aftershocks of pleasure pulsed through our entwined bodies. I wrapped my arms around her, holding her close, savoring the lingering warmth of our connection as we both fought to catch our breath.

"Hunh," she said, her lips pursing against my chest.

"Yeah." I agreed with the assessment I knew was forthcoming.

"That was too quick."

"Far too quick," I echoed. "Can I fuck you with my tongue now?"

"I heard there's a way you can lick me while I suck you."

I raised a brow. "Heard?"

"I saw it in a book. Want me to show you?"

I flipped her body around, placing us in the position she was referencing. I felt her grin against the tip of my cock as I took my first of a million licks at the center of my love.

Her taste was divine, a blend of sweetness and desire that made my head swim. I took my time, teasing and tasting, committed to drawing out her pleasure just as she had commanded mine. Charlotte's moans vibrated through me, fueling my own ardor as her mouth worked wonders below.

We feasted on each other, lost in a world where only sensation mattered. Each caress and lap pushed us closer to the edge of bliss once more. But neither of us was in a rush to get to the end. I was going to take a long time with her. I was going to take forever with her.

Want to read the make up scene?
Don't worry, Charlotte and Jorge are fine.
Its Jorge and Adom that need to heal their broken bromance.
Read the make-up scene in Ines' Reader Group

https://ineswrites.com/ReaderGroup.

ABOUT INES JOHNSON

Lover of fairytales, folklore, and mythology, Ines Johnson spends her days reimagining the stories of old in a modern world. She writes books where damsels cause the distress, princesses wield swords, and moms save the world.

If you liked Ines' Beast then you'll love her Vampires and Dragons. To find out more just visit https://ineswrites.com/ReaderGroup

More PARANORMAL and FANTASY ROMANCE by INES JOHNSON

Dark Vintage
Her Vampire Prince
Her Vampire Lord
Her Vampire Knight
His Vampire Princess

The Last Dragons

The Dragon's Reluctant Sacrifice
The Dragon's Ambivalent Sacrifice
The Dragon's Willing Sacrifice
The Dragon's Rebellious Sacrifice
The Dragon's Compliant Sacrifice
The Dragon's Forbidden Sacrifice